# Thuong Duc

**By**

**Gary K. Cowart**

Cover illustration by Nancy Cowart

Gary K. Cowart



ISBN-10: 1469906244
ISBN-13: 978-1469906249

For my lovely wife Nancy

# CONTENTS

ACKNOWLEDGMENTS

Many thanks to Glenda Minniece, Jeffrey Cowart, and Joy Jarrell for their help and support.

*By the same author*

White Clam
Blood on Red Dirt

# Chapter 1

**Quang Nam Province Vietnam 1968**

Mud caked Cao's boot heals as he sat down on a large gray rock by the edge of the cliff. It had rained heavy the night before and with the NVA probing the wire all night, Cao and his South Vietnamese Ranger counterparts had spent a wet and muddy night.

As he looked over the cliff to the village below, the warm morning sun was sending bright, reflected, streaks of sunlight dancing along the Song Vu Gia River. The surrounding area looked calm, but Cao knew it was filled with danger. The NVA were hiding all around. He wondered if this fight against the communists was worth it. No matter anyway, it was too late to change sides even if he wanted to.

He looked back at the command bunker where the ten Green Berets spent the night dry and warm. He took off his camouflage shirt exposing his thin frame and skinny arms. It was the second day of February 1968, and he wished he could be home in Hoi An for the Tet celebration. However, that had changed two days before with a slew of coordinated attacks by the NVA against every major city in the south.

Cao turned his head and ran his hand through his jet, black hair. He looked east and his eyes caught a glimpse of a Marine walking toward him. It was Corporal Braden. He was one of the Marine artillerymen sent in to support the Special Forces Camp with their 105 mm howitzers.

The Marines were a different lot than the Green Beret advisors. They were younger and more reckless than the Berets, but they were kinder to the people of the village. They laughed and joked and tried to make the best of a difficult situation, and Jim, Corporal Braden, was one of the best of them. He respected Cao and his Rangers and traded cigarettes, candy, and C-rations with them for fresh bananas, rice, and corn. Jim was average height, just less than five foot ten, but still towered over the South Vietnamese.

He was without his helmet and flak jacket, but held his M-16, with two taped together magazines of ammo, tightly in his hands. His mud stained utility shirt was open, showing his muscular features and a good tan.

"Hell of a night last night," Jim said, kneeling down in front of Cao's rock.

"Yes, a number ten bad night," Cao returned. "Many NVA out there."

They both turned their heads west and looked into the mountains, straining to see some sign of the invisible enemy.

"Yea, the bad guys are all around," said Jim. "There's talk of pulling us out soon. What about you guys?"

"No pull out," was all Cao said, still looking west to the badlands.

They sat there in silence for a few moments and watched as the camp came to life. Men were taking off their wet, muddy clothes and cleaning themselves as best they could. C-rations were being broken out, and they could hear laughter from some of the Marines at gun five. Corporal Braden and Sergeant Vien didn't know each other well, but had a relationship because Cao could speak English.

"Say, sergeant, I'm going to see if the lieutenant will let us take a truck down to the river this morning and clean up. Think you could go with us?"

"Maybe."

"I kind of want you to tell Quang about the possibility of me leaving soon. He can understand a little English, but not much, and I want to make sure he knows I'm not leaving by choice."

Quang was an orphan boy that Jim had taken a liking to, and he kept the boy in food and clothes. They had become good friends, and Quang took care of cleaning Jim's utilities and boots whenever he came to the river. Cao had made arrangements for Quang to stay with a widow in the village, and since Jim didn't smoke, he gave his share of the free cigarettes the Marines got to the old woman so she could trade for food.

"Quang will be okay, but I'll talk to him anyway. Either today or next day," replied Cao.

"Thanks, sergeant. I'll let you know after breakfast if we can go to the river."

The river they talked about was not the main river, but a smaller tributary of the Song Vu Gia that fed into the larger river from the north. It ran through the middle of Thuong

Duc, splitting the village into east and west sides. The Song Vu Gia ran from Laos, east to the South China Sea.

*     *

Down in the village the young orphan boy, Quang, was pulling himself out of the sleeping hole under the old woman's thatched bamboo framed bed. He looked around rubbing his eyes, but the old woman was already gone. Their ten by ten thatched hut sat on a bit of a rise in the middle of the village and as such was spared any rainwater runoff. Quang's sleeping hole not only kept him dry and warm, but also protected him against the odd mortar or rocket round that struck the village from time to time.

The boy looked around the dirt floor and into the corners of the hut searching for something to eat, but he had not seen his friend, Jim, for three days, and the last of the C-rations he had gotten back then was gone. He pulled back the cloth door covering and moved outside. The old woman was just returning.

"Good morning, Bian," the boy said, respectfully.

The old woman sat down in front of the hut in a dry spot, her black pajama pant cuffs streaked with mud. She pushed the toes on her dirty feet to flip off her muddy sandals and took two small ears of corn from under her shirt. She tossed one to the boy.

"Here, eat boy," she said, "That's all I could get with the last four cigarettes. Hopefully, you will see the corporal today, and we can get more."

Bian peeled the corn quickly, and her black beetle nut stained teeth bit into the soft sweet corn.

"I hope so, too," returned Quang. "I look for the truck every day. Too much fighting the last two days. Too many northern men. Do you think they will come into the village?"

"It makes no difference boy. We have nothing to give them. Only those with food need worry."

They ate in silence. When the old woman was finished, she sighed, crossed her legs, and sat back against the hut wall.

"The Japanese killed my husband, and the northern men killed my two sons when the French were here," said the old woman. "I hate them for that. I didn't particularly like the French, but they brought us goods we had not seen before. The northern men just bring death."

"Why do they come here? The northern men killed my mother as well," replied Quang. "No one in the village wants them here."

The old woman didn't answer his question.

"If we don't see the corporal we may have to steal rice and corn from the fields at night. It will be dangerous. Go now and look for the truck."

* *

Jim and Cao and some of the Marines were climbing onto the deuce and a half truck. One of the men manned the fifty-caliber machine gun on top of the cab and everyone else locked and loaded their M-16s. Jim and Cao knew the village children would come to the sand bar on the river bank as soon as they heard or saw the truck drive down the hill above the village.

The kids loved the Marines and each one had their favorite. Candy, food, and cigarettes were their reward for cleaning and filling sand bags. It was a ritual that had been repeated time and again over the last two months. The parents of the kids never came around, but it was assumed they stayed away out of fear for the NVA and their sympathizers.

"Okay, we're set," yelled one of the Marines to the driver and the truck started down the hill.

The deuce and a half rumbled slowly down the gravel road that ran from the helicopter-landing zone to the village below.

"Sergeant," Jim yelled above the roar of the truck engine, "I've got this canvas bag full of Newport and Salem cigarettes and some C-rations. Make sure Quang hides them well in case I have to leave."

The truck, in low gear, whined past the first of the village hooches. Cao, eyes still looking west toward the mountains, turned back slightly and nodded okay.

* *

Quang was one of the first kids to see the big truck on the hill belch black smoke as the driver started the engine. Soon he was running to the one lane concrete bridge that spanned the tributary. He got there before the truck did and waited on the east side as other kids gathered around him.

"Jim, Jim," he yelled as the big green truck rumbled over the bridge and made a left turn for the short one hundred meter drive to the sand bar.

Quang took off his green Marine utility cover and waved at Jim and Cao with a big smile on his face, and Jim waved back. The kids followed the truck at a trot, and soon they were all on the sand bar at the north edge of the village. The land was flat with rice paddies and cornfields, and the fifty-caliber machine gunner had a clear field of fire. The fathers and mothers of the children were working the fields with water buffalo and large wooden skids.

"Jim, good you here," yelled Quang.

Jim and the other Marines jumped down from the truck. Cao stayed on the bed with his M-16 in hand.

"Hey, Quang. How you doing?" said Jim, as Quang gave him a waist high hug. "I've got some extra things for you in the truck later."

Quang didn't understand all that Jim said, he never did, but when the good hearted Marine motioned toward the bag on the truck tailgate, he knew there were things in it for him. He grabbed Jim's boots as soon as he took them off and started cleaning. The other boys did the same for their Marines. Cao and the machine gunner kept watch.

"You can do my clothes too," Jim said, as he stripped down to his skivvies. "I'll take a swim and then we'll talk."

Jim waded into the river to about thigh high and launched his well-developed body into a shallow dive. Quang set about cleaning the mud off Jim's utilities and hanging them to dry on the sides of the truck. He put the wet socks and jungle boots on the tailgate and returned to the river bank, lowering himself into a knee high squat and waited for the corporal to finish taking his bath.

Five minutes later, Jim came out of the water and into the warm morning sun. He began drying himself off with his old olive drab towel.

"Hey, kid," he motioned to Quang with his hand. "Come over here to the truck. I got some stuff for you."

"You got C-rats, Jim?" Quang asked, understanding enough to know payment was coming.

"Yeah, and some more stuff too."

Jim saw Cao still scanning the mountains to the west from the truck bed.

"Sergeant, would you tell him the bad news."

No sooner had Cao turned toward the two friends than the first THUMP, THUMP, THUMP of the NVA mortars riveted their attention. They all knew what it was, even the kids.

"Get in the truck ASAP!" yelled Jim.

Marines were running out of the water and grabbing their gear before Jim's command.

"Hurry, HURRY!" Jim screamed.

He turned to Quang grabbing the canvas bag off the truck and shoved it at the boy.

"Go, take it," Jim said. "Go, now, DIDI!"

Didi was the French/Vietnamese slang word for, *go now*, and Quang took the bag and ran for all he was worth, back to his hut and his sleeping hole. The mortars landed up on the hill next to the Special Forces Camp so the children were in no immediate danger.

"Get this truck moving," Jim screamed, and the big deuce and a half lumbered over the bridge and up the hill.

"What the hell are they hitting us in daylight for?" yelled Jim to Cao. "They never hit during the day."

"That's why!" Cao returned. "They caught us off guard."

As the truck turned into the camp mortars were hitting with a regular pace, and the Marines scrambled into the bunkers to take cover and get their clothes on. Jim made his way to the FDC (Fire Direction Control) bunker and started pulling on his pants. Everything was chaos.

"Braden, we got wounded at gun six and we've already called in for a medivac and air support," the lieutenant said. "Get out there and see if you can get me a target."

Jim was an enlisted forward observer and FDC man so it was his job to call in fire missions for the two 105 mm howitzers on the hill. He finished putting on his boots and semi-wet utilities, grabbed his M-16, map, and compass and hustled outside. In the chaos he forgot his helmet and flak jacket.

Smoke and dust were rising from a half dozen places as Jim darted from ditch to bunker, working his way to the cliff. He jumped into a fighting hole and scanned the south side of the river. The mortars had stopped. Things turned quiet. He saw nothing on the south side and moved quickly to the gun six parapet.

"Conner, what's going on?" questioned Jim, as he fell beside the gun six corporal. At the same time Jim noticed three wounded gunners, ten feet away. One looked serious, and the corpsman was frantically working on him.

"I got one guy bad hurt, Sutherland, hit in the chest. Two others with shrapnel in their legs. The lieutenant was here and went to call for a medivac."

"He did! You see where this shit is coming from?" asked Jim.

"I'm not sure. We were just standing around, and they hit. I don't know if they came from across the river like usual; sounded more like it came from the finger ridge to the west."

Jim looked west past the landing zone and all looked quiet except for the Rangers that were on the move refilling their fighting holes with men.

"Connor, where's your land line?" asked Jim.

"Over there, hanging on the breach of the gun."

Jim got up and headed for the phone; he took the earphones and cranked the ringer.

"FDC bunker," Jim heard over the line.

"This is Braden. Let me speak to the lieutenant." Jim said. "Lieutenant, Braden here. I'm at gun six. I couldn't see anything across the river. I'm gonna move up to the landing zone and see what's there."

"Corporal, get the wounded closer to the LZ. Sea Knight choppers are close. Then get back to me."

"Sir, I don't have a radio,"

"I'll send Sandy with a Prick 25, now get going."

Jim set the phone back on the gun and ran low over to Conner.

"Lieutenant says to get your wounded guys over to the LZ. Choppers are close," said Jim. "I'm heading there now. I'll take Pearson and Burkhart with me. They look like they can walk. You'll need a stretcher for your other man."

* *

Quang ran all the way to the old widow woman's hut, clutching the canvas bag tightly. He ran inside and found the old lady sitting on the dirt floor.

"Come here boy. What you got?" she said.

Quang handed her the bag and looked back outside to the hill. The old woman broke open some C-rations and started to eat some pound cake, her favorite side dish. She called to the boy.

"Come here and eat. We are not in danger… yet, anyway. They want the Marines on the hill. Many will die today. The northern men are many. Come eat."

Quang turned back and listened to her. He hoped she was wrong. He worried about Jim. He worried about himself. A tear rolled down his young eyes.

* *

Jim had taken a position at the westward wire next to Cao and his men after dropping off the two gun six men at the landing zone.

"Sergeant, does anyone know where the mortars are coming from?"

"The best guess is west, on the ridge," Cao said.

Just then a blonde, chunky Marine, with a helmet on his head and flak jacket under his PRC 25 radio, stumbled into the ditch. Jim realized at that instant that he was without his body armor. They heard the beat of large helicopter blades as the first Sea Knight drew near the hill. Jim took the handset.

"Red Lima, this is Red Lima Forward, radio check over," Jim called into the radio handset.

"Got you five by five, Red Lima Forward,"

"Red Lima, standby."

Jim turned and watched the Sea Knight make a wide sweep to the north and drop down toward the landing zone. THUMP, THUMP, THUMP. The enemy mortars sang out again. It would only be a matter of seconds before they hit. Jim jumped up to see if he could spot the launch area and saw nothing. The first mortars hit behind and to the right of them.

"Sandy, stay here! I'm going up on that bunker roof for a quick look."

Jim got up and started running toward a nearby bunker whose sandbagged roof was about five feet higher than the ground. As he jumped up on the roof to look for the enemy mortars, it felt like someone hit him in the side with a baseball bat. The next thing he knew, his ears were ringing and his right side was bleeding in two places.

"Jim, you're hit," said Sandy who came running when he saw the mortar explode next to the bunker. "Come on. Get up. The chopper's touching down."

Sandy threw down his radio and grabbed Jim, pulling him to his feet. They both started running toward the open rear ramp of the Sea Knight with the blade wash throwing dust everywhere. Explosions were all around them, as Sandy shoved Jim into the chopper and disappeared back into the dust. Jim was lying on the canvas seat and saw the bullets and shrapnel piercing the thin helicopter skin as the wounded filled the Sea Knight chopper.

"Get this thing off the ground," he screamed, holding his bloody side.

* *

# CHAPTER 2

## TWENTY-FIVE YEARS LATER, MARCH 1992

The cry of the newborn baby boy sent chills of relief through the delivery room as it always did. A large pair of gloved hands gently set the baby into the hands of a nurse who cleared its nose and dried its body. The crying continued as the baby was passed to the mother to hold.

"Looks like a keeper," said the surgeon. "Another boy, third one today."

He took off his glove and combed back the mother's hair gently with his hand. He smiled at her, then turned and walked out. As he left the room and entered the hall his thoughts turned to things other than babies. He continued down the hall and entered the doctor's locker room. Another doctor was there getting ready to start his shift.

"You got your bags all packed, Jim?" the doctor asked while he adjusted his scrubs.

"Yeah. I've got a few things to do this afternoon, and then I'm gone," said the surgeon.

"You know everybody thinks you're crazy."

"Yeah, I know. Why would anyone want to go back there?" returned the surgeon.

"Well, anyway, good luck."

"Thanks, George."

The two doctors shook hands and the second one walked toward the door. He turned back toward his tired friend.

"Hey, kiss one of those hot Bangkok babes for me."

"I'll try and work it in."

Dr. James Braden changed into his street clothes, thinking about the last twenty-five years. His college and medical school, his residency and private practice. His loves and his losses. He knew he was right in doing this. He had no other choice. He had wanted this since the day he left Vietnam on a stretcher with one less kidney and a shot up liver.

Jim walked out of the locker room and down the hallway to the baby-viewing window and took a peek at the three little boys he had helped bring into the world the last few hours. There they were, laying three abreast.

"Gentlemen," Jim said to himself and the babies. "If you only knew what was in store for you, you'd stay right there."

He looked at the babies and his eyes began to water as his thoughts turned to a different place and time.

"I wish you luck, my little men."

Dr. Braden turned and had started down the hallway when he heard someone call, "Jim! Oh, Dr. Braden. You forgot something."

He recognized the nurse's voice. It was Bernice, his oldest friend and trusted colleague. Jim stopped and turned with a puzzled look on his face. He walked back to the older nurse who was dressed in purple scrubs.

"I could have sworn I signed this," Jim said as he took the clipboard from Bernice.

Bernice was standing next to the nurses' lounge door and as she flipped it open she said, "You did. Surprise!"

As he looked through the open door, a group of doctors and nurses and aides were already in prime party mode with glasses raised. Jim walked in to the cheers and greetings of the gathered group. An older nurse gave him a plastic champagne glass full of bubbly.

"Attention please!" said the older nurse. "Everyone quiet… Thank you."

She turned toward Jim and raised her plastic glass.

"Dr. Braden," the old nurse toasted. "Up until a year ago most of us only knew you as a nice, mild mannered, slightly crazy, doctor. We had no idea you were once a war monger and ex-Marine."

Jeers and laughter from the crowd and pats on the back preceded the rest of the toast.

"But seriously," the nurse continued. "Over the years you have come to mean something special to everyone in this room. None of us can begin to understand the feelings you have inside. We can only hope you find what you're looking for on this trip. Farewell, good doctor, safe journey, and a speedy return."

"Hear, hear," commented many in the group as the nurse raised her glass higher, joined by all the others.

Jim took his glass of champagne and drank with the others. He set the glass down and shook hands with many of the guests, making the rounds of the room quickly, as he had other errands to take care of.

"Thank you," Jim finally said to the gathering. "Thank you all, but I have a plane to catch, so I've got to get going. You guys are the best."

Jim hugged Bernice and waved goodbye to the crowd. He took the quickest route to the parking lot, and when he left the building, he felt the first raindrops. By the time he started his Isuzu Trooper he was looking at a downpour.

"I wish I hadn't agreed to meet Hathaway," Jim thought as he pulled out into traffic.

Dr. Hathaway was Jim's therapist and had been helping him deal with his divorce and his Vietnam issues for some months. It wasn't that he didn't like Hathaway; it was just that he knew what he needed to do now, and he wanted to get on with it.

The blue Isuzu Trooper turned into the modest south side medical building and parked at the far end near Hathaway's private office entrance. It had quit raining, but Jim hurried anyway. He wanted to get to the airport early.

Dr. Hathaway was sitting at his desk when the pretty blonde receptionist led Jim inside.

"Jim, thanks for stopping by on such short notice," the therapist said. "I just wanted to make sure that you've thought this trip through. It's only been a few years since the Communists have let ex-military return to Vietnam. It's still a dangerous place, and the US still hasn't got normal relations established yet."

"I know, Doc, but I really need to do this," replied Jim. "Like we talked about before. I left in a hurry. I never had time to make my peace. I want to stand on the spot where I was wounded, and look around in the sunshine. The need is overpowering."

Hathaway nodded, putting his hands on his cheeks thinking. After a short pause he put his hands on the desk and stood.

"Okay, then. You have my number. Call me anytime. Part of me wishes I could go with you. I'd like to see that country myself."

Jim got up and shook Hathaway's hand.

"I'll see you when I get back, but over a beer. I'm done paying your fee," laughed Jim.

Jim turned and walked away, shutting the door behind him. He passed the pretty receptionist, but said nothing. His mind was already ten thousand miles away.

* *

The green cab pulled up to the United Airlines curb in the departure area of Sea-Tac International Airport. The cabby got out and quickly got Jim's baggage, one suitcase and one carry-on. Jim paid the man, grabbed his baggage, and moved inside. It was early in the afternoon and the crowds were light.

Before long Jim arrived at the gate area for his flight to Bangkok. He walked over to a pay phone, picked up the receiver, and started to dial a number. Out of the corner of his eye he noticed a beautiful Asian woman walking his way, and he paused momentarily before finishing the number. His eyes fixed on her face and quickly slid to her tight skirt and high heels. Jim continued to look as she walked by.

Another man, that Jim didn't notice, wearing a dark suit, trailed her at a distance. The man was of mixed Asian descent and had small features and unkempt hair. His teeth were stained yellow and his fingers played with a half-smoked pack of cigarettes in his left coat pocket. He wished he could have a cigarette right then instead of following this woman. Although he noticed the American doctor on the phone and the doctor's interest in this lady he was being paid to shadow, he initially didn't think much of it. Every man stared at her, and he passed Jim by.

Ring, ring, ring!

"Yeah!" an angry voice answered the phone.

Jim was startled back to reality after watching the tall Asian woman pass by. He must have finished dialing the number, but he had been so taken by this striking woman he forgot what he was doing.

"Hey! Is anybody there?" yelled the voice in the phone.

"Yes, I'm here. Larry, Larry Brewster is that you?" answered Jim.

"Yeah, who's this?"

"Larry, it's me. Jim Braden."

"Jimbo!" the voice turned into a happy chirp. "Where are you?"

"Still in Seattle," Jim said. "Listen, sorry I called so early, but I just wanted to make sure you were still okay with picking me up and having me stay with you. I can get a hotel room instead."

"No problem, Jimbo. I got plenty of room. Flight 1175, right?"

"Yeah, that's right. Okay then, if you're sure?"

"Sure, I'm sure. I'll see you in sixteen hours. I'm looking forward to it, buddy."

"Good, well, I'd better get to the gate. You go back to sleep. See you in sixteen hours. Bye, Larry."

Jim hung up the phone and stared at it with unsure thoughts. He wished he could be more enthusiastic about Larry, but Larry was just a little different.

In Vietnam Larry Brewster was in his element, a born mercenary. Larry joined the Marine Corps wanting combat and thrived on it. Jim, on the other hand, saw it as a way to pay for college. They had become friends out of the necessity of war, and had stayed in touch over the years. They were both from poor backgrounds but that's where the similarities ended. Larry was rougher around the edges, a smoker, a drinker, a womanizer, and a live for today type of guy.

Larry never could adjust to being back in the States and had moved to Thailand when Jim was still in college. He had somehow managed to put together enough money to start up a bar in Bangkok and his fortunes grew. He had always wanted Jim to visit, but Jim was busy with school for twelve years. Now he was excited to see Jim, or at least seemed to be.

Jim, on the other hand, wasn't sure he wanted to see Larry, but since he needed to get a Vietnamese visa in Bangkok, he figured *what the hell. How bad can it be!*

Jim picked up his carry-on and started toward his gate. He was getting tired. It was late in the afternoon and he had been up all night delivering the three baby boys. He was looking for a seat in the waiting area and found himself looking for the gorgeous Asian women as well. She was not there.

He found an empty bank of seats and sat down, putting his carry-on on the seat next to him so that no one could sit there. Jim pulled his sunglasses from the bag and put them on. He leaned back and tried to sleep.

* *

Yvonne Chin put her lipstick back in her purse and washed her hands in the ladies' room sink. She was not looking forward to the long flight home. She was tired and stressed from the weeklong business trip, but it had been profitable, and her import-export business in Bangkok would reap the benefits. She was worried about her father, too. She had not heard from him for some time.

Yvonne took her things and walked back out to the waiting area. The small Asian man, reading a magazine and leaning against the wall, watched her go. She looked around for a seat and finally settled on the end seat of Dr. Braden's seat bank. She sat down and looked straight ahead.

Jim was asleep and the movement of the four-seat chair bank when Yvonne sat down woke him. Eyes blurred, he looked to his left and couldn't believe his good fortune. There she was, the striking Asian woman with the legs and high heels to die for. Jim, not wanting to seem too excited, slowly sat upright, took off his sunglasses, and smiled at his new seatmate.

Yvonne made no response and looked straight ahead.

"You going to Bangkok, too?" asked Jim.

Yvonne heard the question, but looked straight ahead. *Great, now this guy is going to hit on me*, she thought.

Still looking straight ahead she nodded.

"I wouldn't be sitting at the Bangkok gate if I weren't traveling there, would I?" she said in her coldest, cruelest tone.

Now Jim was no dummy, and it was quite apparent that this lady was in no mood for an exotic mile-high romance, the wish of every man that ever boarded a plane.

"Sorry, just wondering," he returned.

Jim put his sunglasses back on and slumped back in his seat and pretended to go back to sleep. *Why do the beautiful ones always have to be so bitchy?* he thought.

The small man with the yellow teeth took all this in from his station against the waiting room wall some thirty feet away. To most people, the exchange of words would go unnoticed, but the sinister looking, nicotine stained man was being paid to keep tabs on Ms. Chin and gather information. To him, this quick conversation between the two attractive people seemed more than a coincidence.

"Flight 1175 to Bangkok, Thailand now boarding first class passengers," came the voice over the public address system.

Jim, being long-legged, had decided to pay the extra fare and go business class. He peeked over to Yvonne thinking that this stunning woman was probably flying first class. She didn't budge.

"Flight 1175 to Bangkok, now boarding business class."

Jim got up and to his surprise so did Yvonne. It seemed they were both flying business class. *Oh God, are we sitting together?* thought Jim.

Yvonne was quicker than Jim and moved to the gate a few people ahead of him, but this only served to feed the small man's suspicions and as Yvonne and Jim disappeared into the jet way, he dropped his magazine and headed to the pay phones. The man dialed 0 and waited.

"U. S. West operator," came the voice on the phone.

"I'd like to call Bangkok, Thailand. Collect!" said the little man in a Southeast Asian accent.

* *

**DEEP IN THE NORTHERN THAILAND JUNGLE**

Kai Chin was visibly upset with his situation. All he could think of was destroying years of research and disappearing. They would stop at nothing to get him to continue, but the threats to himself and now his daughter were more than he could rationalize. This was his only choice.

The thin doctor took his white lab coat off and neatly folded it, putting it on the chair.

He looked around the small chemistry lab. It was quite a place to be this far out in the Thai jungle. The palm leaves of twenty different plants waved in the wind outside his window as he began stuffing papers and notebooks from his file into an old wastebasket. He took more papers and packed them into a dilapidated leather briefcase, then closed and locked it. Taking some matches, he struck one and touched it to the paper in the wastebasket. As it burned he retrieved his cane from a hook on the wall and began breaking up the laboratory glassware.

Dr. Chin took his coat, picked up the briefcase and walked outside. He cautiously turned around trying to see if he had been noticed before moving to a muddy Fiat automobile. He got in, took another look around, and drove off into the jungle.

* *

# CHAPTER 3

Larry Brewster moved past the baggage claim area heading for flight 1175's gate. The plane was already starting to unload. He was wearing a bright red and yellow Hawaiian shirt over his expanding belly. The cigarette in his mouth and the gaudy gold chain necklace complemented the stubble of four days worth of beard. He looked anxiously through the crowd of passengers, but didn't see Jim.

As it turned out, Jim did not sit next to Yvonne on the fight, but their proximity made it possible for him to look at her often without the possibility of her noticing. One time during the flight he got up and walked over nearer her seat. They made eye contact and he nodded. She turned away.

As he was getting his carry-on from the overhead compartment, he watched her exit the plane. *It's a shame*, he thought. For some reason he just couldn't shake her image. He resigned himself to never seeing her again, and started off the plane.

Larry was still searching the off-loading passengers when he spotted his old friend. He jumped up and started waving.

"Jim! Jimbo, over here," Larry yelled.

Jim forced a smile and couldn't believe it was Larry. They met and shook hands. A little too vigorously for Jim.

"Larry, is that you? You've put on a little weight the last twenty years," said Jim, all smiles now.

"Shit! Sure it's me, Jimbo. A little heavier, but just as crazy. Damn, it's good to see you. You haven't changed a bit. Still shittin' handsome as ever. It's a wonder you ever got shot, shittin' good looking as you are," exclaimed Larry.

"Well, I was, and they managed to do a good job of it," Jim said. "Where do we go to get my luggage?"

"Come on, this way."

They turned and started to walk. Jim looked around for Yvonne and hesitated for a moment. Once again he was unaware that he was being watched.

"Something wrong, pal?" Larry asked.

"No, nothing. Come on, let's go," answered Jim.

They started to walk again and headed for the baggage claim area.

"Hey, you ever see any of the old platoon?" asked Larry.

"Afraid not," Jim replied. "I lost track of everyone after that last day. If you hadn't have written my mom, I would have lost track of you, too."

"I kept some addresses and wrote a lot of the guys for a while. Some were even thinking of coming over," Larry said. "Mostly to get laid and get away from their old ladies, but no one did until now. Good old Jimbo. Damn it's good to see you."

Larry patted Jim on the back and Jim smiled. *I guess old Larry isn't so bad,* he thought.

They kept walking on past the Vietnamese Airlines booth where an angry refugee family surrounded an old fat man wearing a white, slightly wrinkled suit and a white fedora. The man was Gerald Summerpot, of English decent, born in Singapore years before the start of World War

II. He escaped to French Indochina (Vietnam) where as a young man he survived five brutal years fighting the Japanese. His current capacity was liaison between the Thai government and the Vietnamese refugee movement. Some would say he was less than honest.

"Mr. Summerpot, we have no more money," said the refugee father.

"I realize that," returned Summerpot. "You and your family are out of Vietnam. I have fulfilled my part of the bargain."

Summerpot hesitated, noticing the father's small children. He patted the head of the youngest girl and raised her chin with his finger.

"However," continued Summerpot, "I do know of some employers and other ways to supplement you financially. I'll see what I can do."

Jim and Larry carried Jim's luggage outside the terminal building and approached the nearest cab. Larry motioned to the driver while he lit another cigarette.

"Over here!" Larry yelled. He patted Jim on the back again. "You're gonna love my place."

They got into the cab and settled in for the ride. Larry took a strong puff on the cigarette. Jim was annoyed.

"Those things are going to kill you," said Jim.

"I'm sorry, Jimbo." Larry threw the cigarette out the open window. "That's right! You never did smoke like the rest of us."

"Nope, never did," Jim, said.

Changing the subject, Larry said, "About five years ago things really came together for me. I did some security work for this rich businessman and he floated me a loan for my bar. Since then the money's rolled in."

Listening, Jim said nothing, content to look out the window at the Bangkok night-lights.

"I got a nice apartment above the bar. Two bedrooms and two baths," Larry continued. "And by the way, all my girls know you're coming. They can be a pain in the ass at times, but boy can they screw."

"Girls? What kind of a bar do you run?" asked Jim.

"You don't know? … Larry paused. "Jimbo, this is Bangkok. I run a whore bar. You'll love it."

The taxi pulled up in front of a row of classy taverns and nightclubs not to far from Bangkok's infamous Patpong Road district. The street was busy with tourists, mostly Japanese men, street vendors, and girls pitching the bars. Larry paid the cabby and grabbed Jim's suitcase. He patted Jim on the back once again and headed for the door. Jim looked up at the sign. *Larry's Shanghai American Bar.* Larry turned back.

"Come on in, Jimbo,"

Jim followed Larry through the front door and immediately Jim was impressed with his first look. The place was not as sleazy as Jim had imagined when Larry called it a whore bar. It looked anything but that. A good looking thirty-something man dressed in a black suit and tie came to meet them.

"Hey, Matty, get over here," Larry called.

"Hello, boss," said Matty.

"Matty, this is my old Marine Corps buddy Jim. Jim, this Matty."

"Nice to meet you, sir," said Matty.

Jim nodded and they shook hands. "Pleasure's all mine," said Jim.

"How we doing so far tonight?" asked Larry.

"We got a good start. The rising sun is shining."

Matty's quip about their Japanese clientele was not lost on Jim. He looked around the beautiful bar noticing the many Asian businessmen and the pretty and very young Thai, Malay and Burmese girls draped in nice dresses and high heels. Matty handed Larry a clipboard which he read and then signed the document.

"Larry, I'm impressed. This is quite a place," said Jim.

Larry smiled at Jim as two drop-dead gorgeous Asian girls walked over to them, one taking Larry's arm and the other moving next to Jim.

"Is this Dr. Jim?" said the first girl to Larry.

"You doctor, Jim?" said the second in more of a thick accent.

"Jimbo, you devil. Shit, you're a hit already," smiled Larry. "Go ahead take her. Take them both. Hell, sometimes I do three or four at the same time."

Jim was obviously embarrassed by the sexual attention, and as the young girl at his side stroked his thigh, close to his groin, he couldn't help but be aroused.

"Look, Larry. This isn't the place or the time for this," Jim said quietly.

"What? It's a whore bar, for God's sake," returned Larry. "It's legal … Twenty-four hours a day. Loosen up Jimbo. Don't you like them?"

"Well, yes. They're beautiful, but …"

"But what?" Larry interrupted.

"Don't you worry about AIDS?" asked Jim.

"Shit no! My girls don't have that crap!" said Larry. "They get checked once a month!"

"Larry, I'm a doctor. That's not how AIDS works."

"Hey! It's good enough for me. Besides both of us should have been dead twenty-five years ago …"

Jim stared at Larry and flexed his eyebrows. Larry shrugged.

"Okay, girls. Give Jimbo a break. Let me show him around and get him drunk. You can have your way with him later."

Larry kissed and hugged both girls before they walked away. They both waved goodbye to Jim.

"Look, Larry. I didn't come here for a sex weekend, although I'm struggling with that now. I've got other things on my mind …

I appreciate the thought though… By the way, checking the girls monthly doesn't work. It can take months for the HIV virus to sero-convert and show up on blood tests."

"Jimbo, you worry too much. While you're sero-converting, I getting some serious prime ass. Loosen up for Christ's sake … Come on. I'll show you the dining room. You hungry? Want some food?"

The two men entered the dining room, which was even more impressive than the bar. It was a real five-star restaurant. A few couples were sitting at tables eating a late dinner. Jim's thoughts turned back to the two beautiful Asian girls and maybe he may have been a little too stuff-shirted.

Larry and Jim sat down at a table with exquisite linen and highly crafted chairs. A waiter dressed in a white shirt and black bow tie greeted them with water and coffee. Everyone in the place was a direct contrast to Larry.

Larry was looking at the menu and didn't immediately notice Jim's surprised look when Yvonne Chin entered the dining room through the main street entrance and sat at a table in the corner.

"I don't believe it," said a surprised Jim.

Larry looked up and saw Jim's expression. "Believe what?"

"The girl from my flight." Jim paused. "Now if I was interested in women tonight, and I'm not sure I am, that's the one I would like to be with."

Larry turned and looked into the corner.

"Who, that broad? She's bad news. She probably screws like a two-by-four. You know, just lays there without moving. Besides she's too old. You need a hot twenty-year-old."

"Too old," Jim disagreed. "She can't be much over thirty; thirty-five at the most! And what do you mean, she's bad news?"

"She's a rich bitch. A snob. She owns some kind of an antique store. Does some import-export bullshit," Larry said.

Just then Matty walked in the dining room and walked over to Larry. He leaned down and whispered something in his ears. Larry turned and looked back at the entry door and whispered something back at Matty.

Jim couldn't hear what was being said, but he was mesmerized by Yvonne Chin and didn't much care. She looked up and noticed Jim. They made eye contact, and Jim nodded. She was surprised to see him again and looked away.

Larry stood up. “Jimbo, excuse me for a minute. Business.”

Jim watched as Larry went with Matty to the front of the dining room where he met and shook hands with an impeccably dressed Chinese man in his late twenties. The two exchanged words a few moments before the Chinese man headed for Yvonne’s table with Larry following.

The Chinese man had a less than happy expression on his face, and when he passed Jim, the expression turned to a cool stare. He continued to the table where Yvonne was waiting. She acknowledged him, and he continued to stand while they talked. Larry returned to Jim’s table.

“Who’s the guy, her boyfriend?” asks Jim.

“Hardly. His name is Chi Woo. Thinks he’s a big man in town... So, Jimbo, what can I get you? Chicken, steak, cheeseburger?”

“Cheeseburger?” Jim questions.

“Yeah! We got everything here.”

Jim heard raised voices from Yvonne’s table and turned to see Chi Woo and Yvonne arguing. The man grabbed Yvonne by the arm and when she threw his hand off, her purse fell to the floor, spilling some contents.

"Your friend doesn't seem like a nice man," Jim said, staring at the young Chinese.

"Leave it be, Jim." Larry warned.

Chi Woo grabbed Yvonne's arm again, this time with some force, and she cried out.

"Let go, you bastard! I didn't come to this awful place to be treated like this," Yvonne screamed.

"Where is your father, Miss Chin?" returned an angry Chi Woo.

Jim started to get up, but Larry restrained him, grabbing his wrist.

"Jimbo, it's not your concern."

"Larry, it's okay, I just want to introduce myself."

Jim shook off Larry's grip and got up. He walked over to the table, placing himself between Chi Woo and Yvonne. He towered over them both. He didn't look at Chi Woo, but talked and looked at Yvonne instead.

"Excuse me, miss. Did I hear you speak English?" Jim asked.

Chi Woo was still holding Yvonne by the arm.

"Fuck off," said Chi Woo, staring at Jim.

Jim turned to face Chi Woo. A broad smile appeared on his face.

"Oh, I see you speak English as well." He turned back to Yvonne. "I hope you have a more acceptable English vocabulary."

"Hit the road, Joe," Chi Woo replied in his Chinese accent.

"The name is Jim, not Joe."

Larry moved closer to Chi Woo. Jim stared back at Chi Woo and without turning back addressed Yvonne.

"Miss, do you wish to continue conversing with this gentleman?" said Jim, keeping his eyes in contact with Chi Woo.

"Absolutely not!" was Yvonne's reply.

Chi Woo dropped Yvonne's arm and started to reach for his inside coat pocket when Larry gently grabbed his hand and arm from behind.

"Perhaps it's time to leave, Mr. Woo," said Larry with blunt determination. He extended his look as if he had some control over Chi Woo. They stared each other down, and Chi Woo suddenly smiled. He turned back to Yvonne.

"Another time then, Miss Chin. Give my best to your father when you see him."

Chi Woo bowed slightly to Yvonne, then faced Jim squarely, still smiling, but with a sinister overtone. "And you, sir. I hope to see you again as well," said a smiling Chi Woo.

"My pleasure," Jim nodded and continued smiling himself.

Chi Woo turned to leave, giving Larry a cold stare. He walked off with Larry following behind.

"Here, let me help with your purse," said Jim as he knelt down.

"It's not necessary," said Yvonne, kneeling to pick up her belongings.

Jim found a loose pile of business cards and slipped one into his pocket before handing the rest to Yvonne. She was stunning, and he felt a strong attraction this close to her. After gathering the rest of her things, she stood up and addressed Jim.

"I want to thank you for your intervention," said Yvonne.

"No problem. May I join you? Miss Chin wasn't it?" asked Jim.

Yvonne hesitated this time for she saw something in this American that appealed to her, but she had so many things on her mind. He was kind and seemed nice, but she had met men like that before who turned out to be controlling and abusive. Still, somehow he seemed to be different.

“I’m sorry, I’m not staying. This place wasn’t my choice for a meeting anyway.”

“Please, just one drink. Besides, you need to let that guy get out the door and away from here,” said a concerned Jim.

Jim pointed to the front entry where Chi Woo and Larry were still engaged in a firm conversation. They didn’t seem happy with one another.

“Listen, Woo. Don’t cause trouble in my place, and don’t push me,” Larry was saying. “I have friends in town, too! Now GO! You can deal with her later. My friend is leaving for Vietnam in a few days, maybe sooner.”

“You know, Mr. Brewster, some people, in this city would rather see you go instead,” replied Chi Woo.

“Beat it, Woo.”

Chi Woo smiled again, bowed slightly and left.

Yvonne looked annoyed, but thought maybe it was best to give Woo some time to leave the area.

“Yvonne,” said Yvonne, out of the blue.

Jim was caught off guard. He had expected her to decline, but now he had hopes of her staying a while.

“Pardon me?” he asked.

“My name. It’s Yvonne. Yvonne Chin,” the beautiful woman said.

“James Braden,” Jim said, not sure why he used his formal first name. Maybe because he thought it would impress her. He shook her hand. It was cold, but soft. It was thrilling. “Yvonne Chin? That’s Chinese. You don’t look Chinese. In fact I’m at a loss to put my finger on exactly where your ancestry might be.”

“I’m not Chinese. Well, that’s not totally true. Part of me is. It’s a long story.”

“I’ve got time and I’d love to hear it,” Jim replied.

Yvonne was becoming anxious and fidgety.

“Look, James. I don’t want to be rude, but I must be going. Thank you for your help,” said Yvonne, as she picked up her things and walked out, leaving Jim mystified and completely intrigued with her. Yvonne passed Larry as he returned to Jim.

Jim took the business card out of his pocket and looked at it. *Y. Chin, Antiques, Import-Export, and Asian Treasures.* He put the card back in his pocket as Larry reached the table and sat back down.

"Someone ought to teach your friend some manners," said Jim.

"He ain't my friend!" returned Larry. "Jim, there are things in this town that are different than back home. That babe is definitely bad news. Stay away from her for your own good."

Larry's serious expression changed back to all smiles.

"Come on. Let's order some food, have a beer, and then get some ass."

* *

**THUONG DUC VILLAGE, VIETNAM.**

An old dilapidated panel truck drove up the crowded dirt road as villagers moved to the side, letting it pass by. It came to rest at a hillside bamboo and concrete hut, adjacent to many other huts, and crowds of cautious, village elders surrounded it.

The double back doors of the old truck swung open and Dr. Chin, the Asian chemist, got out and was greeted warmly by the gathered men. He was taller than his Vietnamese hosts and looked different from them. It was obvious that he was a man of respect and importance in the village and was treated so. An older lady, the village matriarch, greeted him, and, after bowing to her, he was hurried inside the hut.

*　*

# Chapter 4

The bed covers were thrown back on the empty bed and there was the sound of water coming from the small bathroom next to the hallway. Jim walked back into the bedroom wiping his hands on a small towel. He threw the towel on the dresser and straightened the bed somewhat, then found his wallet and sunglasses. He drew back the window curtain. It was a sunny day. He expected nothing less.

He picked up a Seattle Mariners baseball hat, placed it on his head and as he moved back out into the hallway, he passed Larry's room. The door was half open, and Jim couldn't refuse a look. Larry was still asleep. There was an empty fifth of whiskey on the nightstand, and the two naked Asian girls were intertwined and asleep with Larry on his bed.

Jim chuckled to himself and smiled. His own night passed alone thinking of Yvonne Chin. His senses told him she was danger, but his common sense said she was not to blame.

The American doctor left by the private entrance, walking out into the sunshine. The street was busy and chaotic with morning traffic, mostly the small golf cart-like *tuk-tuk* taxis and motor scooters. Pollution and burnt oil clouds filled the air.

Jim adjusted his sunglasses and hailed a passing tuk-tuk. The taxi pulled up to the curb and the driver popped his head out of the doorless cab. He was all smiles, and as Jim started to speak the cabby's smile turned to alarm.

"Hey, Joe! Watch out!" yelled the cab driver.

Jim felt two sets of strong arms grabbing him on both sides, pulling him back to the building. He tried to resist, but a third man appeared and punched him in the stomach. Jim doubled over, losing his cap, and the three, young, Asian men slammed him up against the wall of the *Shanghai*

*American Bar*. While the first two thugs held him, the third thug pulled back his head by the hair and put a knife blade to his throat.

"Mind own business, Joe!" said the knife-wheeling thug.

He punched Jim in the stomach again, and the three ran off down the street. Jim slumped to the sidewalk. The tuk-tuk driver ran over and helped Jim to his feet.

"You okay, Joe?" said the driver.

"The name's Jim. Yes, I'm okay. I just don't take a punch as well as I used to. You speak English?"

"Oh, yes. Pretty good, darn well, okay," replied the driver. "You want nice gold ring?"

Jim was taking inventory of his body, checking for broken ribs and the like and found none.

"No, no rings. I need to get to the Vietnamese Embassy … or maybe a hospital." Jim felt the throb of pain in his gut. "You know where it is?"

"Hospital?"

"No, the Vietnam Embassy," said Jim with lingering pain.

"Oh, yes. I know pretty good, darn well… Okay Joe, I take."

The taxi driver headed back to his taxi as Jim straightened up. *Joe? Do I look like a*

*Joe to everyone?* he thought to himself. Jim got into the back of the tuk-tuk, and the driver drove out into the busy downtown street.

A few cars back a late model Mercedes sat at the curb. Chi Woo and another man sat in the back watching Jim pull away in the tuk-tuk.

"Go now. Keep up with that taxi," Chi Woo said to the driver of the Mercedes.

The luxury car pulled out and followed the tuk-tuk, winding through the streets of Bangkok. Jim was feeling better and surmised his early morning meeting with the three young toughs was a direct result of his interaction with Chi Woo and Yvonne the night before. It was personal now, and Jim wanted to find out just what this situation entailed.

Before long the tuk-tuk taxi stopped in front of a large jewelry store. The Mercedes stopped a few doors back.

"Okay, Joe. You want gold ring?" said the driver as he got out on the sidewalk.

"What I want is the Vietnamese Embassy. What the hell is going on here?" Jim demanded.

"My uncle, he own store. I get you very, very good price. Okay Joe?" said the driver.

Jim smiled, realizing that he had been conned. Just as he was about to tell the driver to move on he noticed the antique store next door. He pulled the business card out of his pocket remembering Yvonne was an antique dealer.

"Hey, I tell you what," said Jim. "I don't want a ring, but I would like to go to this antique store."

He handed the card to the driver. The little man frowned and moved his hand gesturing in a so-so motion.

"I want to go there," said Jim.

"Go here?" The driver points at the card.

"Yes!"

"Maybe so. Okay, I try pretty good, darn well. Okay, Joe.

"The name's Jim."

The driver got back in the cab and they started out once more. Jim was wondering what all this extra driving was going to cost. Chi Woo followed, in the Mercedes, curious to see where Jim was going. It didn't take long. The taxi pulled up to the curb and Jim read the sign on the storefront.

*Y. Chin, Antiques, Import-Export, and Asian Treasures.*

The two men got out of the tuk-tuk and went up to the antique store door. The Mercedes pulled up a few cars back.

"See, I told you," said Chi Woo to his companion. He was more suspicious then ever of Jim now.

Jim and the taxi driver entered the store. The woman clerk behind the counter was very pretty, but it was not Yvonne. The driver went to the counter and spoke to the clerk in Thai.

"I have brought you this rich American tourist, and I expect a ten percent commission on anything he buys," said the driver.

"Ten percent!" returned the clerk in Thai. "This shop does not work that way. You'll be lucky to get ten percent of my commission, if anything at all."

"Okay, I can live with that," said the driver.

"Fine!" the clerk replied.

Jim hadn't understood a word they had said, but he could tell there was a negotiation going on.

"Okay, pretty good, darn well, Joe. You look, I get good price," smiled the driver.

Jim chuckled and started looking around the full racks and tables. He picked up a stone statue, a Buddha figurine, and casually walked over to the counter.

"Nice statue," Jim said.

The clerk smiled, but before she could say anything Yvonne walked out of the back room. She was dressed to kill, showing her long legs, heels and dark pantyhose. Jim did a double take. She was different today with reading glasses on and her hair pulled back in a ponytail. She was reading an invoice and didn't notice Jim standing there. She spoke to her clerk in Thai.

"Did you find that …" Yvonne noticed Jim and paused, mid-sentence.

"Good morning," said Jim.

Yvonne handed the paperwork to her clerk and sized up Jim. She was not sure whether she was glad to see him or not.

"Hello. Can I help you find something?" Yvonne said matter-of-factly.

"Well, actually I didn't want to buy anything."

Yvonne's expression and tone became short.

"Look, mister ….whoever," Yvonne started.

"Braden, James Braden," Jim helped her remember, using his formal first name again thinking it sounded more impressive.

"James." Yvonne took a deep breath. "I'm thankful for last night, and I'm flattered by your attention, but I'm a busy woman, and you do not interest me socially. I'm sorry if that offends you, but you need not waste your time."

Jim was taken back a notch and grabbed for words.

"Ah, I'm sorry too …ah … I just thought you were an interesting woman. I thought maybe you would accept an invitation to show me your city and have dinner tonight."

Yvonne realized how short she was. She didn't want to hurt his feelings. Another place, another set of circumstances and maybe … maybe, but not now.

"I'm sorry, too," she smiled. "I have a lot on my mind. If I can ever help you with antiques, just let me know."

"I can see I made an error in coming here," replied Jim.

Yvonne smiled a little bigger and turned to leave. Jim called to her.

"Excuse me. There is one thing you could help me with," said Jim.

Yvonne stopped and turned back, still smiling.

"What's that?" she said.

"You could tell me how to get this taxi driver to take me to the Vietnamese Embassy," said Jim.

"Vietnam Embassy? You wish to travel to Vietnam?" said Yvonne, with a spark of interest.

"Yes, it's the reason I came here to Bangkok, to get a Vietnamese visa," returned Jim.

Yvonne stepped closer. "You've been there before?"

Yes, during the war. I would like to go back to the village …" Jim hesitated, not wanting to say he was wounded. "Well, I would just like to go back where I was at during the war. A small village in the hills west of DaNang, named Thuong Duc."

Yvonne gasped, visibly shaken. She composed herself quickly. Jim knew he had struck a chord.

"You've heard of it?" he asked.

"Yes. Yes I have … Yvonne composed herself. "Why do you wish to go back there?"

Jim knew he had touched on something that interested Yvonne, and he wanted desperately to find common ground with this woman.

"If you're really interested I could tell you over lunch."

Jim gave her a hopeful look. Yvonne hesitated momentarily. She smiled.

"Okay, you win, James. I suppose we can have lunch," surrendered Yvonne.

"Good, now you can help me get to the embassy."

Yvonne followed Jim and the tuk-tuk driver outside to the curb where they got back in the taxi.

Down the street, Chi Woo and the other menacing man looked at each other as they watched Yvonne and Jim converse.

Yvonne said goodbye to Jim and turned to the tuk-tuk driver. Her demeanor changed and she spoke in Thai.

"Now, take him straight to the Vietnamese Embassy. Stay with him and watch him every minute, and then bring him back here. I want a report of his actions. You're working for me now. Understand!"

The driver nodded.

"You will be paid well."

"Yes, madam," said the driver in Thai.

Yvonne turned back to Jim.

"You shouldn't have any more trouble with this driver. He will be at your disposal the rest of the morning and will bring you back here. It won't cost anything. My treat for helping last night," Yvonne said.

"Thanks, I'll get lunch," Jim returned.

"Until then," Yvonne smiled.

The tuk-tuk drove off, and Yvonne stood a moment watching it leave. Her smile turned to a troubled look as she walked back into her shop. She didn't notice the Mercedes, with Chi Woo inside, pull out into the street to follow the taxi.

Yvonne walked past the counter and didn't talk to the clerk. She went to her back office and picked up the phone. As she dialed she tried to make sense of all that was happening. The phone rang and a voice answered.

"It's Yvonne … we may have a potential problem … an American … I don't know, he was on a flight with me from Seattle. He is interested in Thuong Duc …no, don't tell him yet… yes I will."

She hung up the phone and stared at the wall. *What is he up to?*

The tuk-tuk came to a stop in front of the embassy in cloud of blue smoke. Jim wondered if any car in Bangkok had an engine that didn't burn oil. He got out of the taxi and leaned down to the driver.

"I assume you are going to wait. I'm not sure how long this will take," said Jim.

"Okay, Joe, no problem," said the driver.

As Jim started to walk away, he noticed the driver getting out and following him. He stopped, and the driver stopped too.

"No," Jim said. "You wait here."

"No problem, Joe," returned the driver.

Jim started again and the driver followed. Jim hesitated and started to say something, but figured, *what's the use,* and continued on. The Mercedes was still a few doors back at the curb. Chi Woo wasn't a patient young man, but he wanted to make sure of his facts before he acted again.

Inside the embassy Jim found groups of refugees standing in lines, waving papers, and shouting at the officials. It was general chaos as Jim tried to make his way through the crowd and find someone who spoke English. He reached a counter where he got the attention of a Vietnamese clerk.

"Excuse me. Sir, do you speak English?"

The clerk gave Jim the once over and replied.

"I speak a little English."

"Good. Where can I get an entrance visa to Vietnam?" Jim said.

"Where you from?"

"United States," Jim said. "I'm an American."

The clerk looked coldly at Jim like he'd never seen an American before.

"You have American cash dollars?"

"Yes. Many cash dollars," said Jim.

"Second floor, room three," said the clerk.

Jim turned to go to the staircase and bumped into the tuk-tuk driver. He shuffled past the driver and they both went upstairs. Jim looked around and the driver tugged at his shirt. The driver happily pointed out room three. Jim looked at him not sure what his game was.

"Thanks," said Jim.

They both turned and entered the room. There were no lines of refugees only a single clerk behind a counter with a desk. A second door beyond the counter connected the room with other offices.

"Excuse me, sir. Is this where I can get an entrance visa?" Jim asked.

The clerk looked confused and replied in Vietnamese.

"I don't know what you are saying. Go downstairs and petition for an interpreter."

"Great! He doesn't speak English," said Jim.

Jim looked at the tuk-tuk driver at his side.

"You don't speak Vietnamese, do you," he asked.

"Maybe so. I try darn good. Okay, Joe?"

"Yeah, right!" Jim looked around the room and then started for the hallway.

"Not many people traveling to Vietnam these days,' said a voice behind Jim.

Jim turned around and saw a fat man in a white suit standing in the side doorway. The man stepped closer and offered his hand.

"My name is Summerpot, Gerald Summerpot. Maybe I can be of service? You have a passport?"

Summerpot mumbled something to the Vietnamese clerk. Jim took out his passport and handed it to the fat man.

Outside, Chi Woo was growing impatient. He had been sitting in his Mercedes all morning and was ill at ease. He turned to his henchman, his mood getting worse.

"Go in the embassy and see what's going on," Chi Woo said.

The henchman got out of the Mercedes and headed for the stone steps at the foot of the embassy. He eased passed the guard and through the door. Going inside he looked for

Jim in the mass of standing people. Looking into every doorway and coming up cold, he noticed the stairway and moved to the second floor. It didn't take long to find Jim talking to Summerpot, a man the henchman knew well. He ducked out of sight, but stayed nearby where he could keep track of the situation.

"There you go, Dr. Braden, a fourteen day visitor visa," said Summerpot. "Remember, you must have only United States currency, and you must keep an exact accounting with receipts for items purchased. The black market is very big on American money."

Jim took the paperwork and put it in his wallet. He offered his hand and shook with the fat man.

"Thanks, Mr. Summerpot."

"Here, let me walk you out, my friend," added Summerpot. He took Jim's arm and moved him to the hallway. The tuk-tuk driver met them at the office door and followed them down the stairs. Chi Woo's man followed also.

"Nasty war, that American affair," Summerpot said, as he walked Jim down to the first floor. "Never should have happened. All it accomplished was to make a lot of rich men richer and a lot of poor men dead."

Chi Woo's man was able to move past the fat man and the doctor and arrive at the front door first. He left the building and quickly rejoined Chi Woo in the back of the Mercedes. They talked briefly and Chi Woo took a car phone and dialed a number. He shouted a few words into the phone and hung up.

Summerpot, Jim, and the tuk-tuk driver walked out into the sunshine and stood on the steps.

"You know, my friend. I am due to go back to DaNang very soon myself," said Summerpot as he wiped his brow with a handkerchief. "Perhaps I can speed up my departure and meet you there. Do you gamble?"

"I play a little a little poker," replied Jim. "Nothing serious."

"I know a place near China Beach. Very discreet. Gambling is supposed to be illegal, but if you know the right people, they tend to look the other way. You might humor me with a game."

Down the street an old green truck, trailing blue smoke, made its way along the busy avenue. A man sat in the passenger side and cocked a semi-automatic weapon.

"Well, then I hope to see you in DaNang," Jim said. "I might need some help. Thanks again."

Jim and the driver started down the steps toward the sidewalk and the parked tuk-tuk taxi. They didn't notice the old truck or the window rolling down or the gun pointed in their direction. They started to get in the taxi as the truck pulled by.

BLAM! BLAM! BLAM! The shooter fired three shots in quick succession at point blank range. Both men ducked, but surprisingly the shooter missed, his bullets striking the stone steps and flying harmlessly elsewhere.

Summerpot lumbered down the steps fearing the worst. The driver got on his feet first and helped the doctor up.

"You okay, Joe?"

"Yeah, I guess so," replied Jim.

The fat man arrived out of breath. "Dr. Braden! Are you all right?"

"What the hell is going on? Those guys tried to kill us," said the angry doctor.

Summerpot gave Jim a look of skepticism. He noticed the Mercedes drive by with Chi Woo in the back, plainly visible, and gave the young gangster a look of recognition. Jim, dusting himself off, didn't see Chi Woo.

"On the contrary, my friend. I believe they were only giving you a message," said the fat man in all seriousness. "If they wanted to kill you, they would have."

Jim cleared his mind and thought over what Summerpot just said. He was right. It was point blank range. First the mugging, now this.

"Yvonne," Jim said, thinking out loud.

"I beg your pardon?" asked the fat man, not understanding what Jim had said.

"Oh, nothing. It's nothing."

Jim gazed down the street. He motioned to the driver to get going and said goodbye to Summerpot.

Jim was fuming now. Getting punched was bad enough; getting shot at was the last straw. It took only a short time to get back to Yvonne's shop. Jim jumped out of the tuk-tuk before it came to a full stop and barged in the door of the antique store, passed the clerk and some customers and went directly into the back office. Yvonne, sitting at her desk, was startled to see Jim. Jim got close, right in her face.

"Listen, lady. I admit I was attracted to you before, but now I'm just curious. Who the hell are you, and why have I been used as a target and a punching bag the last three hours?"

Yvonne got over her initial surprise and calmly answered, "James, please sit down."

Her perfume permeated the air, her eyes dug into him. If it wasn't love at first sight, it was surely lust in the first degree. Her calm manner made him pause. He sat down.

"James. Your life is in danger, I believe, through no fault of your own," Yvonne continued. "I suggest that you cut short your visit and return to the United States."

"I might just do that! You mind telling me why?"

"I'm sorry you felt obligated to act on my behalf. All I can say is you have been seen in the wrong place at the wrong time. Please go. Perhaps you can visit your village another time. Vietnam is still a dangerous place. More so than here."

Jim shook his head in disbelief.

"You're right, Miss Chin. I will cut my visit in Bangkok short and leave as soon as possible, but I have business in Vietnam. Important business. I'm sure it doesn't concern you or your problems here. Good day, Miss Chin."

Jim turned and left the store thinking about the day's events and hating the fact that he was leaving a woman who had raised such desire in him. Desire he had never known before. Outside the antique shop, Jim saw a beggar woman with four little kids sitting next to her. He shook his head at her, and dropped some Thai money in her can.

"Do yourself a favor, lady, and stop having kids."

She smiled a toothless grin and was very happy not knowing what he said. Jim walked back to the tuk-tuk and got in.

"Where to, Joe?"

"To the airport, then to the Shanghai American Bar ... and the name is Jim!"

The tuk-tuk driver took Dr. Braden to the airport where he got a ticket on the only Vietnamese Airline flight to DaNang the next day. After returning Jim to the Shanghai American Bar the driver got money from the doctor and then proceeded to Yvonne's antique store to report and get paid again.

Yvonne was now convinced that Braden was an innocent bystander in a dangerous game, but she had no way of convincing her enemies of that. She decided that she must follow him to Vietnam, in part to see that he stayed out of trouble, and in part, well, she wasn't sure why.

Later that night Larry and Jim were having dinner in the bar dining room. Larry was stuffing himself with food. One of the bar girls came over to deliver two more drinks. He patted her on the butt.

"Thanks doll…Shit, Jimbo," Larry said between bites. "I told you that babe was bad news…. Shot at, beat up…the dumb broad! First time a buddy comes over here and this has to happen."

Jim toyed with his drink, thinking about Yvonne and this whole situation.

"It's definitely not what I expected…Well, I'm out of here tomorrow. I just wish I knew what was going on."

Larry paused between mouthfuls, his tone becoming more serious. "It's not your concern, pal." Larry paused again, then continued. "Look. Maybe she's right. This Chi Woo fella is connected. When you crossed him, you may have pissed off some important people. I think it's a good idea to head on to DaNang. These people don't fool around…Maybe this will resolve itself by the time you get back. You keep your nose clean, and I'll meet you there in a couple of days. Then we can go back to the old village, get drunk, laugh a little, cry a little and forget about all this."

"It'll be a long time before I feel like laughing about this. And that friend of yours, Chi Woo! I'd like to slip him an M-79 for breakfast," said Jim.

"First of all, he's no friend. And second of all, stay away from him. It's like fuckin' with the Mafia, for Christ's sake."

Larry paused again, and leaned over to pat Jim on the back again.

"Forget about it. Forget the broad. She ain't worth it."

Jim stared, thinking about Larry's words. The sexy Thai waitress brought another round of drinks for them. Larry looked long and hard at her as she walked away.

"God, I like skinny asses." He turned back to Jim. "You like skinny asses? That's what you need, my friend, before you're too old to enjoy it."

Jim chuckled and shook his head. Good old Larry. He'd never change.

* *

# Chapter 5

Jim Braden was leery of the Vietnamese Airlines Russian-built airliner he saw in front of him. First of all it was small, and second of all, as he left the terminal for his short walk to the plane, he noticed the tires looked bald. Now at the bottom of the portable stairway, Jim stared at the plane and fear rose in the depth of his body.  He looked at the under belly of the plane and saw what looked like bailing wire holding a lower compartment door closed. He looked up and saw the paint peeling off the top of the fuselage.

As he stepped up the stairway, he was conspicuously taller than everyone else.

The Vietnamese Airline area of the terminal building didn't have a first class waiting room, so Yvonne found a corner window in one of the many bars. It happened to afford a view of the plane, and she watched as Jim started the boarding procedure. Dressed in a traditional Vietnamese, Ao Dai, or silk dress, broad hat and sunglasses, she looked every bit a Vietnamese woman.

Inside the hot plane, Jim was making his way down the crowded aisle, hugging his carry-on briefcase and bag. Most all of the other passengers were Vietnamese and were quite a bit smaller than Jim. He excused himself as he struggled past each row of people trying to settle into their seats.

"Excuse me, … excuse me, please."

He finally reached his row and checked his ticket. He was horrified to find that it was the middle seat and the seats were so close together that he knew he wouldn't fit well in the small space. Two Vietnamese men occupied the aisle seat, and window seat, already.

Jim pointed to the middle seat.

"That's my seat. Do you speak English?" he asked the man in the aisle seat.

The man just glared at Jim. Jim looked up and found the overhead bin full with bags and goods. He tried to get into the middle seat holding his briefcase and bag, but he couldn't do it.

"Excuse me, could you take the middle seat and I can hang my legs into the aisle," he said to the man in the aisle seat. "Do you speak English?"

The man didn't speak English, but through a bit of crude sign language Jim was able to convince the annoyed man to move over. Jim crammed himself into the aisle seat with his knees practically touching his chin and his bag in between, obviously uncomfortable. He smiled weakly at his neighbor who was now even more annoyed. Jim heard a voice speaking his name.

"Dr. Braden!"

Jim looked up and saw Mr. Summerpot looking at him from down the aisle.

"Perhaps you would like to join me in first class, such as it is," said Summerpot.

"Mr. Summerpot, yes, is there more leg room?" Jim replied.

"Yes, my man. Not much, but better than back here."

Jim struggled out of the chair and gave his neighbor a little bow and a thank you. He moved quickly toward the front, and the fat man led him past a curtain into the first class seating area.

"I was able to free up my calendar and leave for DaNang earlier," said Summerpot. "Here, let me take that bag. The first class décor is the same, but the seats are further apart, and the Hanoi beer is free."

"I tried to get a first class seat, but they said all were taken," Jim explained.

"No matter, my boy," said the fat man. "They always keep an extra seat for me. Sometimes the company of a lady friend makes the flight more tolerable."

Jim and Summerpot settled into their roomier but still humble seats as Summerpot said something to the attractive attendant. As the attendant left, Yvonne entered the cabin. She took the seat across the aisle from Summerpot and bumped him slightly.

"Pardon me, madam," the fat man said.

"Please, it was my clumsiness. Forgive me," Yvonne replied.

Jim turned at the sound of her voice. He was once again, struck by her overwhelming beauty. Yvonne, thinking Jim was in the coach area was surprised he was sitting with Summerpot.

"Miss Chin?"

"Dr. Braden. How nice to see you again," said Yvonne.

"You two know each other. How splendid. Would you like to sit next to one another?" asked Summerpot.

Jim smiled at Yvonne. "I don't think so. Strange things happen to me when I'm around her," said Jim.

Yvonne smiled under her sunglasses. Summerpot turned from one to the other, picking up on their mutual attraction.

"How charming!" said the fat man.

* *

An older, impeccably dressed man sat at a desk, in a darkened room, on the Bangkok waterfront, smoking an Asian water pipe in the dim light. The outline of another man was visible in the shadows behind the desk. Chi Woo entered the room and addressed the old man.

"Kai Ling, I have news."

"Have you found the old man?"

"No, but…"

"I want the old man found," interrupted Kai Ling. "Each day without him costs the cartel a fortune. The time of reasoning is past. Where is the girl?"

"That is the news I have to tell you," continued Chi Woo. "She and the American doctor have boarded a flight to DaNang. The fat man is with them."

"Have your people found any relatives or friends of the old man?"

"No."

"Then pick up the girl and hold her in DaNang. Put out the word on the street. I'm sure the old man wants her to live. Word will get to him."

The man behind Kai Ling was restless and shuffled the distinctive pair of shoes on his feet. The shiny brass ornaments on the loafers were all Chi Woo could see.

"And what of the American?" Chi Woo asked.

"Kill him if he gets in the way again!"

"As you wish."

Chi Woo nodded to Kai Ling and bowed. He smiled at the hidden man as he slipped out the door.

* *

On approach to DaNang, Jim watched the co-pilot come back to first class and open a trap door in the aisle floor. He was taken back when he could see daylight under the trap door. The co-pilot proceeded to crank the landing gear down by hand. Yvonne and Summerpot seem completely at ease with the situation so Jim kept his mouth shut. Summerpot eyed him.

"Nervous, my boy?" said the fat man as they started their final approach.

Jim glanced at Summerpot with a quizzical look. "It's a little unnerving to crank the gear down by hand." The plane was almost down, passing other planes lining the edge of the strip. "And those Russian Mig fighters lining the runway don't help," continued Jim.

The plane taxied to the terminal building and the portable stairway was positioned against the plane. The door opened and the first class passengers exited first. Yvonne stepped out, followed by Summerpot and then Jim.

They headed into the building and Yvonne and Summerpot, obviously recognized, were waved through customs by the Communist guard. As Dr. Braden followed, he was stopped abruptly, almost rudely.

The guard spoke to Jim in Vietnamese.

"I'm sorry, I don't understand you," said Jim.

Summerpot stopped and called back from the other side of the counter.

"He wants you to put your bags down and show your passport," the fat man yelled.

"Oh, here you go."

Jim set the bags down and reached into his coat pocket for the passport. He handed it to the guard. The guard read it for a few seconds and then the guard looked up with a cold stare.

"U.S.?" the guard said.

"Yes," Jim answered.

Jim began to feel uneasy and wondered whether it had been smart to return after all. The guard started going through Jim's bag and pulled out a group of old pictures showing a younger Jim Braden sitting on the back of a Marine jeep with his arm around the young Vietnamese boy, Quang. The next picture was of Jim and Cao standing on the Thuong Duc ridge holding their M-16s. The guard looked at Jim, then back at the pictures.

Jim was quite sure the guard had never seen anything like this before and he showed them to his companion guard. They both looked at Jim this time and motioned to the picture.

"You? In war?" said the second guard.

"Yes," Jim replied.

The guard spoke in Vietnamese and put the pictures back in the bag. The first guard stamped the passport and gave the passport and bag back to Jim. He said something in Vietnamese and motioned Jim through.

"Thank you," Jim said, as he gave a little bow.

While Jim was being questioned, Summerpot had waited, taking a liking to the American; he now took Jim by the arm and walked him out of the terminal building into the glaring, hot sun. They walked over to the taxi stand where Yvonne had been waiting.

"Which hotel are you staying at my dear?' asked Summerpot.

Yvonne turned and raised her sunglasses like she didn't know who was talking.

"Why, the Green Plaza," she said.

"I should have known, it's the only decent hotel," the fat man said, turning and speaking to Jim. "And you, my boy?"

"Well, I'm staying at a different place," answered Jim.

"Nonsense, my boy! You'll stay with us at the Green Palace! We'll share a taxi. My treat."

Jim waited for Yvonne to object, but she said nothing. The fat man and Yvonne got in the back of the next taxi and Jim rode in the front. Soon they were speeding in and out of the mostly bicycle and scooter traffic and before long pulled up to the Green Plaza Hotel, situated on the west bank of the Han River.

The three companions got out amidst a sea of people. People everywhere were crowding the sidewalks. A policeman came over and yelled at the cabby to move out quickly. Jim watched the exchange.

"What's the matter? Is there a problem?" Jim asked.

"I believe there is a bicycle race about to begin. The officer wants the cab moved before the racers approach. Bicycle races are very popular," Summerpot said. "I see them here all the time."

Yvonne was suspicious of everyone and was not sure if she had met this fat man before.

"You seem to know a lot about Vietnam. With all my travels here, I'm surprised we haven't met before," said Yvonne.

"A man of many talents my dear … I would have remembered such a beauty had we met before. Now you must allow me to treat you both to dinner. No excuses, I insist!" said Summerpot.

Yvonne and Jim looked at each other as if hoping the other would agree.

"Perhaps Dr. Braden would rather I not attend?" said Yvonne.

"On the contrary, I can't wait to see what life unfolds for you at dinner. It's fine with me," said Jim.

"It's a date then. I'll make reservations for seven o' clock." The fat man turned to go inside leaving Yvonne and Jim a moment behind. Jim extended his arm like a gentleman.

"Maybe we can start over again. New town, new time?"

"James. I'm here to look at antiques. Maybe I can help you with your village, but that is all."

Yvonne turned to go inside, and Jim was left on the sidewalk alone except for the thousand people waiting for the bicycle race.

*  *

The thatched grass and bamboo hut was dark and cool. The chemist, Dr. Chin, sat with a circle of men on the earthen floor. The village matriarch handed him a ceremonial bowl of rice. They exchanged smiles. The chemist was pleased and took a mouthful of rice with his fingers. The gathered men smiled, and he handed the bowl to the next man.

* *

Jim checked in and found that Summerpot had arranged for the room already. The desk clerk called the other hotel and cancelled Jim's reservation. It was only for one night at a cost of ten U.S. dollars and Jim had them go ahead and charge his credit card. The Green Plaza was nice, better than he expected, and for only twenty dollars.

Hearing the cheers from outside, Jim decided to look at the race. He walked out of the hotel into the sunny sidewalk filled with people watching the race. A few cyclists sped by to the cheers of the crowd. Jim could see just fine since he was almost a foot taller than everyone else. He moved closer to the curb and smelled an open street sewer.

The lead group of racers was nearing the hotel for the second lap and one man at the back of the pack was older and was riding an older bicycle. He was laboring badly to keep up, and his clothes were old and torn. He was barefoot as well. Just before the cyclist reached Jim, his front tire popped with a BANG! The man screamed a warning as he lost control and the people scattered to avoid him. Jim moved too late as the bicycle crashed into him.

Both men tumbled to the sidewalk in a tangle with the bicycle lying in the open sewer and sewer debris splattered over Jim's clothes.

"Son of a gun. Shit!" exclaimed Jim.

He pulled the dazed cyclist off his lap and looked at him turning his nose up at the smell of the man's hands and face, which had ended up in the sewer. The crowd roared with laughter around them. The cyclist shook his head.

"Shit! Shit! Shit!" said the cyclist.

"Yes, that's what it is alright," Jim agreed. "Hey! You speak English."

"Sure, I speak good. … You're American!" said the cyclist.

"Yes," replied Jim.

"Soldier?" said the cyclist.

"Yeah, well, Marine actually … Aren't you a little old to be riding in a bicycle race?"

The cyclist sat up and checked his teeth, then took a long look at Jim and smiled.

"Just trying to pick up some quick cash," said the cyclist. "What the hell you doing here, Joe? You need a guide? I have a cab."

"I should have guessed."

By this time Jim figured every cabby called Americans, Joe. Jim helped the man up as a group of four other Vietnamese men in their forties ran up. They were dressed in rags and barefoot, too. They fussed over the cyclist making sure he was all right.

"These are my friends. You need to go anywhere, I take. Make you good deal, special for American Marine. I haven't seen a Marine in twenty years," the cyclist said.

"Yeah, and you were probably shooting at him," returned Jim.

"No, no. No VC. We all Rangers," said the bicycle man, as he waved his hand around his friends. "We not communists, we South Vietnamese Rangers. Me sergeant and squad, at your service."

The sergeant turned toward his men and spoke in Vietnamese.

"This man was U. S. Marine."

The sergeant smiled and saluted Jim; his men did the same. Jim, not sure what to do, made a mild attempt at a return salute, then took the sergeant's hand and shook it.

"My name is Jim, Jim Braden."

Mr. Summerpot was standing at the hotel door looking for Jim. The crowd was disbursing as the race had come to an end.

"Dr. Braden, there you are."

The fat man walked over to the group of men. As he drew near the stench of the sewer made him turn his nose initially, then he recovered.

"Mr. Summerpot. What can I do for you?" said Jim.

"I've been looking for you, Jim. What happened to you?" said Summerpot, as he noticed the smelly stains on Jim's clothing.

"Just a little biker problem," said Jim.

"Oh, well, I thought we might go to the local police station. I have a friend that can help you get the travel permits you need," said Summerpot.

"We know police station. We take you cheap. You wait here Jim. Be back in a minute," said the rag-tag sergeant.

The former sergeant turned and yelled at his squad of men to get the cabs and turned back to Jim for approval.

"Okay. Go ahead. Do you mind, Mr. Summerpot?"

"Goodness gracious, no, my boy," returned Summerpot.

"Thanks, Mr. Summerpot. I can use the help," said Jim.

"So can your cabby friend."

"Kind of a motley crew, aren't they. You'd think they could earn enough money to buy some decent clothes," said Jim.

"My dear Dr. Braden. It has been some time since you've been here. Those men make pennies a day if they're lucky," said Summerpot.

"Why so little? They have cabs don't they. No one else looks that ragged," returned Jim.

"Wait until you see their cabs. They don't own them, they rent them," said the fat man. "You see, when the communists took over in 1973 the men who fought for the South were considered traitors. Many were put to death. Most were put in prison and just recently released. They lease their cabs for a high price and realize a very small return. Not a very good situation considering most of those men are still loyal to an American government that abandoned them. It's the only job they are allowed to do."

Jim was at a loss for words as the sergeant and his squad returned, each pedaling an old rusty, dilapidated pedi-cab. Jim looked surprised and disappointed.

“That’s the cab.”

“You bet! You pick, all good,” said the former sergeant.

The sergeant was all smiles; he swept his hand toward the assembled cabbies. They all jumped off and dusted their cabs, smiling and trying to please.

“How much to the police station?” Jim asked.

“One hundred dong each,” replied the sergeant.

Jim turned to Summerpot with a puzzled look.

“About twenty-five cents. I can have a motorized cab here very quickly if you prefer.”

“No. I guess that’s a bargain. Besides I feel I owe it to them. Here…” Jim handed the U. S. dollar to the sergeant. We’ll take two cabs. This ought to cover it,” Jim continued.

“Thank you, sir. We get change later.”

“No need. Keep the change,” replied Jim.

Jim got into the sergeant’s cab and Summerpot into another. After an exchange of glances between Jim and Summerpot, and an order yelled by the sergeant, the whole group of five cabs peddled away.

As the cab squad moved out, a forbidding looking man folded a paper under his arm and watched the group leave before disappearing back into the hotel.

The pedi-cabs rode side by side through the busy streets full of people and produce. They passed a clothing stand with American jeans and tee shirts on sale and a sign that said, *Levis*.

"How are you enjoying the ride," yelled Summerpot.

"Actually, it's a nice afternoon. This is quite pleasant," Jim responded.

They soon pulled up to a two story stone building. Jim and Summerpot got out. The fat man headed for the main entrance, while Jim lingered momentarily. He turned to the sergeant.

"I don't know how long this is going to take. Do you mind waiting?" said Jim.

"No problem, Jim."

"By the way, we really only need two of you. The others can go," commented Jim.

"No problem, Jim. We all stay. They like you. We take turns driving you," the sergeant said.

The men all smiled at Jim. Seeing as how they were all staying, Jim shook his head in wonder. He turned to go, then stopped, and turned back once more.

"All right. If all of you insist on staying around, take this money and go buy some decent clothes. Is twenty enough," asked Jim.

"No, Jim. We can't take this."

"Go ahead. You earned it a long time ago. It's not a handout. Take it."

Jim extended his hand with the twenty-dollar bill.

"I'll need a lot of cabs the next few days. I saw some American clothes down the street. Hurry up now, before I change my mind."

"Thank you, Jim."

The sergeant was touched.

Jim turned and headed for the door. *That's probably the last I'll see of those guys*, Jim said to himself. He turned back one last time.

"Hey, bring me a receipt," he yelled.

As Jim walked inside the police station he saw Summerpot and a policeman talking in a back cubicle. They seemed to be annoyed with one another at first, and then they became almost secretive in their talk, taking quick glances at Jim. Finally Summerpot pointed toward Jim and his scowl turned to smiles as he beckoned Jim back to the cubicle.

"Dr. Braden, back here."

Jim continued back past the busy office workers.

"Dr. Braden. This is Captain Tran Minh of the DaNang police," said Summerpot.

They shook hands. The captain eyed Jim with some suspicion and displeasure. Jim's clothes still stunk. He noticed the captain's revulsion and tried to explain.

"Oh, I had an accident with a bicycle a while ago. It was kind of messy," Jim said, as he tried brushing himself off.

The captain was immaculate. Not a hair out of place and his uniform neatly pressed. He was tall for a Vietnamese, and his mustache was trimmed to perfection.

"Dr. Braden. I hear you wish to travel to the western part of the province," said Captain Minh.

"Yes, to the village of Thuong Duc."

"Why do you wish to make such a dangerous trip?" continued the captain.

"I'm not sure myself. Closure, I guess."

"Closure? What does this mean?" asked the captain.

"I left so quickly twenty years ago…I want to stand on the spot where I was wounded. Reflect on the past. Get some healing. That's closure, I guess. I'll know when I get there," related Jim.

"I see. Closure. I think I understand. Mr. Summerpot told me you were here during the war. I was but a young man myself... Well, that was a long time ago. I must warn you that there is no shortage of weapons left over from the war, and the countryside has been known to harbor bandits. The mountain people do not trust those of us from the coastal cities. I could not guarantee your safety."

"Perhaps I could help!"

The three men turned at the sound of Yvonne's voice. She was radiant and impressively dressed, looking confident and beautiful.

"Miss Chin. How nice to see you once again," said the captain, obviously taken with her beauty and just as obviously lusting after her body.

Tran Minh took Yvonne's hand in his and kissed it tenderly while looking up into her eyes.

Jim could feel himself fume under the skin. It was a feeling he had not experienced in some time. Not since his divorce, years earlier, had the bite of jealousy hit him like it had now. It was more than just her beauty. He couldn't explain it to himself how he felt, he just knew that every time he saw her walk into a room his heart pounded, his hands got sweaty, and he was lost in her gaze.

Yvonne took her hand back and forced herself to not look at Jim. Deep inside she was enjoying the attention Captain Minh was displaying, not for herself, but for how it must make Jim feel. She knew she was attracted to the American doctor, she just didn't understand why it had happened. Their worlds were so far apart.

"Captain, how nice," Yvonne said.

"So, Miss Chin. You are familiar with this village, are you?" said Summerpot in a suspicious tone.

"I have collected antique items at that particular village in the past," answered Yvonne.

"I see, interesting my dear. I was once there myself, many years ago…" Summerpot reflected. "Tran, why don't you assemble permits for all three of us. Miss Chin and I should be able to keep Dr. Braden from getting wounded a second time."

They all chuckled slightly, but Yvonne was surprised and suspicious that Summerpot was inviting himself along. She did not trust him and would rather keep as many people away from Thuong Duc as possible.

Jim, on the other hand, was grateful for Summerpot's help and was pleasantly surprised about Yvonne's plans to accompany him.

Captain Minh was more interested in keeping Miss Chin in DaNang. He was somewhat of a womanizer and his lust for the Eurasian beauty came with no honorable intentions. He had no choice, but to let her finish her travels and then he could have his way later.

"Very well," said Captain Minh. "The government official, Lieutenant Nguyen, is the man in charge of the Thuong Duc district. Dr. Braden, that camp you were wounded at is now a government facility. Lieutenant Nguyen has the final word for permission to enter the area."

Tran Minh grabbed some paper and a pen. He wrote hurriedly and concisely.

"Here, this note should help you," said the captain as he handed the paper to Jim.

"Thank you, captain," said Jim.

Captain Minh nodded his acknowledgment.

"It will take a few hours to process your travel permits. I'll need your passports. I can drop them off at your hotel later."

"Splendid," said Summerpot. "As chance would have it, I'm already treating Miss Chin and Dr. Braden to dinner. Can you join us?"

Jim could have killed the fat man for that invitation. Tran however looked at Yvonne longingly.

"I'd be delighted," he answered.

Captain Tran Minh walked Jim, Yvonne, and Summerpot out of the station and into the bright afternoon sunshine. As they walked out they were making small talk until Jim abruptly stopped and stared ahead. The other three looked with shocked gazes as well.

"What the…" Jim said.

The cab sergeant had the squad assembled in front of their cabs. They were all wearing new red T-shirts and colorful Bermuda shorts. All five men were holding a can of Coke Classic in their left hand while saluting with their right. All the T-shirts were the same style with bold lettering in English on the front: *LIFE'S A BITCH, AND THEN YOU DIE!*

"Attention!" said the sergeant.

The men finished their salute with a snap of the hand and came to attention. The sergeant smiled at Jim. Jim couldn't believe they had come back much less spent the money on clothes.

"We bought American clothes. Okay, Jim?"

He handed Jim a piece of paper and some change in Vietnamese Dong.

"Here is receipt and change. We got very good deal."

"Where did you get those?" Jim asked.

Yvonne and Summerpot were amused and couldn't keep from laughing. Captain Minh was not pleased in the least.

"Black Market!" the sergeant said, indifferent to the police captain. "Many American goods in Black Market…. Say what does *BITCH* mean?"

Jim turned to Yvonne and Summerpot, and they all had a hard time keeping a straight face.

"Take your pick of the cabs. The ride back to the hotel is on me."

The cab squad smiled.

*     *

A waiter carried a plate full of broiled fish with the heads and tails still attached to the table where Summerpot, Captain Minh, Yvonne, and Dr. Braden were seated. Their meal was half over and Summerpot was eating heartily with a linen napkin stuck in his collar to protect his white suit.

"On the contrary, my dear boy," he was saying as he looked over the new plate when the waiter set it down. "Vietnam has never been a truly communist state. Take Tran's family for example. During the war with the Americans, he spent more time working in his father's capitalistic café then he did as an intelligence officer. Again I say the war was not needed."

"But Ho Chi Minh wanted to turn all of Southeast Asia into a communist dictatorship," returned Jim.

"And what is happening to the communist dictatorships in Europe?" continued Summerpot.

"Communism is failing," said Jim.

"Exactly my point doctor," said Summerpot. "It's failing all over the world, and it would have failed here sooner or later with less bloodshed."

Captain Minh lit a cigarette and took a long drag. He eyed Jim and then Summerpot.

"Dr. Braden. Pay close attention to Mr. Summerpot's words. He was here during all of World War II. He met Ho Chi Minh. Ho was a nationalist first and a communist second."

The waiter started to clear some of the dishes as the meal wound down. Jim turned to the waiter before answering Captain Minh.

"Excuse me, there's a group of cab drivers outside at the curb. Could you box up the leftover food and see that they get it?" said Jim.

The waiter looked to Captain Minh and he nodded approval and spoke to the waiter in Vietnamese. The waiter turned back to Jim.

"Yes, sir"

Summerpot wiped his face with the linen napkin, leaned back in his chair, pulled out a Cuban cigar from his inside coat pocket, and started to caress it with the bottom of his nose. Yvonne broke her silence.

"Mr. Summerpot. If you were here at the end of the war you must know that the people that succeeded your friend Ho put many Vietnamese nationals to death instead of trying to embrace all Vietnamese."

"Thank you, Miss Chin for being on my side," said Jim.

"Touché, my dear. However, I did say less bloodshed, but bloodshed none the less," said Summerpot.

"Vietnam is a country of nationalists and capitalists waiting to explode. Once the United States normalizes relations, democracy will not be far behind, but you didn't hear that from me," added Captain Minh.

"Let's hope so," said Yvonne.

"Well, enough of this serious talk. Anyone for desert?" asked Summerpot.

"Not I," said Yvonne.

"By the way, here are your travel permits and passports. I almost forgot to give them to you," said the captain, as he passed out the paperwork to Yvonne and Jim. "Yours as well, Mr. Summerpot."

"What about this poker game I've been hearing about. Is it still on?" asked Jim.

"Please, Dr. Braden, not in front of the good captain," smiled Summerpot.

Jim realized that Summerpot said gambling was illegal and felt he had compromised the situation.

"You mean I'm not invited," said the captain.

"Of course you are," returned Summerpot. "If we get arrested, you can bail us out."

They all laughed looking at Jim as he realized everything was okay.

"Poker, I wonder," said Yvonne.

"Why yes, my dear. Do you play?" asked Summerpot.

Yvonne pondered the question and looked at Jim.

"Perhaps!"

* *

The terminal building at DaNang airport was dimly lit as Chi Woo, in a dark blue suit and tie, and patent leather shoes, entered the building from the tarmac outside. Two local Vietnamese thugs in open collar shirts and slacks, with flip-flops on, walked forward to meet him.

"Where is the girl?" Chi Woo asked.

"The Green Plaza Hotel," said the first thug.

"Good! Let's go," replied Chi Woo, never breaking stride as he continued down the airport corridor with the two thugs following.

Chi Woo had a dislike for Vietnam and the Vietnamese people and enjoyed feeling superior.

"Get my bags," he ordered the second thug, handing him the baggage claim ticket. "Where's the car?"

"This way, Mr. Woo," answered the first thug.

*   *

Summerpot walked out into the warm evening air followed by Captain Tran Minh. He noticed the cabbies on the curb eating the leftover food from dinner. The captain took a cigar Summerpot offered and lit it. Jim and Yvonne soon followed.

"Tran, since it is only a few blocks away maybe we could trouble you for a ride to the club in your car," said Summerpot.

"Wait," said Jim. He called the leader of the cabbies over and the former sergeant joined him.

"Thank you for the food, boss. You want go somewhere?" asked the cabbie.

"Yeah, get the squad ready," answered Jim.

Jim was in no mood to put Yvonne in close quarters with the captain and wanted the cab squad instead. Captain Minh was annoyed. Yvonne noticed a little girl crying on a doorstep some feet away and walked toward her.

"Captain," said Jim, "Why don't you ride with us? My treat. You can have your car follow. It would boost the self-esteem of my friends to have you ride with them. It seems they have suffered for many years."

Captain Minh looked suspiciously at the ex-ranger cabbies and fiddled with his cigar.

"Dr. Braden. I must warn you that some of our citizens may not look kindly on your actions concerning these men. I think I shall retire to my own car for now," replied the captain.

"Maybe it's time for a change," continued Jim.

"Maybe so, but not tonight. Are you coming Mr. Summerpot?"

"Yes, I prefer the auto. Just let me tell this cabby where we are going."

Summerpot told the cab drivers where to go and returned to Jim.

"I'll meet you at Madam Lee's," said the fat man. "Miss Chin, are you coming?"

Yvonne was kneeling down on the steps with the little girl who was still crying. She was straightening the girls long black hair and trying to console her.

"You go ahead. I'll come with James, besides I can't stand cigars."

Tran Minh was visibly annoyed now and threw away his cigar as he entered the waiting auto. He was guessing he was losing influence over Miss Chin to Dr. Braden and was not happy. He was never happy when anyone came between him and a woman he had in his sights. Summerpot kept his cigar and the car drove off.

Jim walked over to Yvonne and looked at the little girl. Memories of all those Thuong Duc kids came rushing back. Those smiling faces of the little girls when all around them death and destruction presented a dreary life.

"Are you hurt little one?" Yvonne asked in Vietnamese.

"No, but I want my mother," the little girl answered.

Jim took a seat on the steps next to the little girl. He looked into Yvonne's eyes and then at her kneeling body. She was so beautiful on the outside, and now he was seeing how beautiful she was becoming on the inside.

"What have we here?" asked Jim.

"James, she's lost, poor thing," said Yvonne with motherly passion.

"Lost? … Her mom must be around here somewhere close," said Jim.

Jim looked around for the cab leader and called him over. He ran over and knelt down next to Yvonne.

"Hey, sarge. By the way what is your name?" asked Jim.

"Name Cao," said the cabby.

At the sound of his name Jim had a brief moment of recognition, a feeling of déjà vu. He quickly let it pass.

"Cao, see if the squad can find her mom. Will you?" said Jim.

Cao jumped up and yelled an order in Vietnamese sending the cab squad in different directions.

"You have a tissue in your purse?" Jim asked Yvonne.

She opened her small purse, took out a tissue and handed it to Jim. He took the little girl's head and gently tilted it toward him, wiping the tears from her eyes. Yvonne was somewhat surprised and watched Jim in a dreamy state. She was beginning to see another side of him as well; a side of him she was happy with. A side that made her feel better about her attraction to him.

"I tell you what, young lady. Do you like cartoons? You know Mickey Mouse?" asked Jim.

The little girl looked confused and as Jim took a pen and small notebook out of his coat pocket, he realized she couldn't understand him.

"Come on, Miss Chin, help me out here," said Jim.

Yvonne snapped out of her trance and spoke to the little girl in Vietnamese.

"Do you like cartoon pictures?"

The little girl said nothing, but had become more interested in Jim. She leaned nearer Jim and watched as he drew a picture of Mickey Mouse. She recognized the world famous mouse and a broad smile formed on her face.

"Cam, Cam!" came a call from down the street.

Jim and Yvonne turned to see the little girl's mother running toward them with the cab squad in close pursuit. Jim quickly tore out the cartoon and handed it to the little girl as her mom swept her up in her arms. She embraced her daughter and the little girl showed her mother the cartoon. The mother bowed and thanked Jim and Yvonne and walked away with her little girl, babbling in Vietnamese.

“Boss, we should go now,” Said Cao. “Not good to keep police chief waiting.”

“Right!”

Jim got up and took Yvonne’s hand in an effort to help her up. She accepted gladly and kept the contact with the doctor’s hand a beat longer than normal. He did a double take and smiled at her.

Jim and Yvonne got into the two cabs that Cao pointed to and the whole squad moved out as one.

A moment later an older American automobile pulled up to the curb in front of the Green Plaza and Chi Woo got out.

* *

# Chapter 6

Chi Woo and his two henchmen walked down the hallway to Yvonne's room. They had a frightened hotel clerk with them. Chi Woo knocked, but no one answered.

"I told you she isn't here!" said the clerk.

"Open it," ordered Chi Woo.

"I can't do that. It's against hotel rules," returned the clerk.

The thug directly behind the clerk clipped him sharply on the head with the back of his hand.

"Mr. Woo say open door."

Now the clerk was really frightened and without any further ceremony opened Yvonne's room. Chi Woo walked in and turned on the light. He walked over to the bed and looked at the open suitcase. He picked up some lingerie and threw it back down. After checking the bathroom he returned to the clerk.

"Where is the woman?" asked Chi Woo.

"I'm not sure. She had dinner earlier with the police chief and two white men. Then they all left," answered the clerk.

Chi Woo waited a moment and came closer to the clerk. He grabbed the clerk's tie and started to straighten it.

"Where did they go?"

The clerk was very uncomfortable and looked back at the two Vietnamese thugs before answering.

"I heard talk of Madam Lee's at China Beach, but I can't be sure. They may have gone elsewhere. I have no reason to lie to you," said the nervous clerk.

"Good man, I believe you," Chi Woo said. "From now on make it your business to know where she goes and with whom."

"Yes, sir."

"Take this as a retainer."

Chi Woo put a US five dollar bill into the man's shirt pocket and patted his chest.

*   *

Cao and the cab squad sat in their empty cabs outside of Madam Lee's club laughing and joking at their good fortune. The police car was a few feet away with Captain Minh's driver waiting patiently inside.

Inside Madam Lee's an attractive Asian cocktail waitress made her way through the club's main room. The room had the feel of Las Vegas on a cheaper and smaller scale. Blackjack, dice, and roulette tables crowded the center as smoke rose in great blue clouds above every table. The gamblers were many and noisy.

The waitress entered a private room through a wide, open doorway, partitioned with rope beads. A small lady, Madam Lee, sat at a table with Summerpot and Captain Minh on either side of her, while Jim and Yvonne sat across. She was older, but like many Asian women she had kept her looks and her petite size. She was always happy to have the police captain visit and paid him good to look the other way, both in money and other benefits.

She had survived the war playing both sides against the other and had never stopped.

Her club had made her a very wealthy woman and very desirable as well.

“Mr. Summerpot, how much did you say a Dong is worth?” asked Jim.

“About three hundred and seventy Dong to the U. S. dollar,” answered Summerpot.

“Let’s see that would be over fifty bucks,” Jim figured. “Okay, I guess I’ll stay for 20,000 Dong.”

“I fold,” said the captain.

“I’m sure someone has bettered my very low two pair hand,” said Summerpot. “I fold as well.”

Yvonne looked at Summerpot and then at Jim and smiled. She looked at her hand again and shifted her cards. She looked at Madam Lee and then at Jim again. She threw in her cards.

“I’ll let James and Madam Lee decide it,” said Yvonne.

Madam Lee looked at Jim and smiled.

“Well, Dr. Braden. It seems as though you have to beat three queens.”

She laid out her hand for all to see. Jim looked at her hand and smiled back.

“Well, hmm…that’s a pretty good hand! What’s a few thousand lost Dong among friends?"

Jim threw his cards in, and they all laughed as Madam Lee gathered in the money. A man with a distinctive crooked nose walked by the door and stopped momentarily. Yvonne noticed him through the bead ropes. She waited a few seconds until he was gone then started to get up.

"I think I'll sit this hand out. Pardon me Madam Lee, where is the ladies room?" asked Yvonne.

"Next to the cashier's booth, dear."

"Thank you."

As Yvonne rose from the table, Captain Minh stood as a courtesy. Jim made an attempt at standing only after Tran did, and Summerpot was content to make no attempt at all. All eyes watched her shapely figure as she walked out of the room.

"Interesting young woman," commented Madam Lee.

"Indeed," said Captain Minh.

He continued to stand and watch her, and Jim felt a jealous stab again. Summerpot's intuition sensed that both men were attracted to Yvonne and fearing a contest between the two, decided to change the subject.

"You know, my boy, I, too, have been to this village you so anxiously seek. And might I add, in a similar situation," said Summerpot.

"You were at Thuong Duc?" returned Jim.

"Precisely! I was a young man, not even twenty, working in the rice exporting business in Singapore, my hometown. I was born to English parents. Being of an adventurous nature, I relished the opportunity to come by ship to DaNang on a temporary assignment. As luck would have it, I arrived a week before the attack on Pearl Harbor. We tried to get a ship back to Singapore, but the Japanese Navy made that impossible, and shortly Singapore fell to the Imperial army.

Things looked bleak, and after the Japanese invaded this country - it was called French Indochina then - I fled west with a Vietnamese friend who had relatives in Thuong Duc. Before long I found myself learning the Vietnamese language in earnest and also found myself consorting with a group of young nationalists, who hated the French and the Japanese both. Most of the French left when the Japanese came and I was soon fighting the Japanese occupation."

"That's fascinating! Is that where you met Ho?" asked Jim.

"Well, no. Ho at that time was a world traveler. He had worked his way on ships and came to live in the United States before I was born. Most people don't know that. He studied in England, France, China, and the Soviet Union before returning to Vietnam in 1941. He was fifty years old when he formed the Viet Minh. He fought the Vichy French and the Japanese and was supported by the U.S. government during the war. In 1944 United States OSS doctors treated him for malaria, and that was where I met him. I had been wounded and needed a delicate removal of a Japanese bullet. The OSS doctors help me with that at the same time they treated Ho. Our meeting was brief."

"I had no idea about Ho's connection to the United States," Jim said.

"Most Americans don't. Its true Ho was a Marxist, but if President Harry Truman would have supported Ho after the war instead of the French, well, things would have been much different the last thirty-five years," related Summerpot.

"But Vietnam would still have become communist, right?" asked Jim.

"Yes, but for how long? With U. S. support, a nationalist like Ho would have seen, as the Russians later did, that communism is at best a transitional government," continued Summerpot.

"Hmmm. Interesting perspective. And did you return to Thuong Duc after your wounds healed?" asked Jim.

"Yes. I stayed in the Thuong Duc area until the war's end."

"So we both lived through different wars in the same village, twenty-five years apart and meet twenty-five years later. Truly amazing," said Jim.

"War holds many strange stories," said Madam Lee.

"Indeed!" Captain Minh broke in. "What if I told you two that you're not the only ones here tonight who lived through a war in Thuong Duc."

Jim and Summerpot looked at each other in confusion.

"But my friend, it can't be you or Madam Lee. You're both from the north," said Summerpot.

"No, not Madam Lee, or me!" said Captain Minh. "It was Yvonne!"

* *

Yvonne walked through the main gambling room heading for the restroom and looking for the mysterious man at the doorway. Halfway there she saw him and gave him a nod. He looked around and followed her toward the restroom hallway. Outside the ladies' room Yvonne waited for the man to join her. He stepped into the hallway and cautiously greeted her, handing her a note without saying a word. They both looked around and seeing no one close by Yvonne read the note quickly. However, their precautions were not good enough as one of Chi Woo's thugs recognized Yvonnc from his place at a blackjack table. He saw the two enter the hallway and quickly returned to report to Chi Woo who was waiting outside in the car.

"Very, well," she told the man.

She scribbled something on the back of the paper and handed it back to the man.

"Take this to my father. Tell him he is in danger and to prepare to leave at once. I will leave for Thuong Duc within the hour," said Yvonne.

The man nodded and left while Yvonne went into the ladies room.

The man left the club, walking past the cab squad and the police car. Cao watched the man, thinking he looked familiar in an odd sort of way. Then he remembered the crooked nose. He had seen that man somewhere in the past, the long past, but could not place him.

The man continued past another auto and headed down a deserted street. Chi Woo and his two Vietnamese thugs were in the auto watching him pass by.

"That man!" said one of the thugs to Chi Woo. "The one with a crooked nose. He's the one that met with her."

"Are you sure?" asked Chi Woo.

"Very sure!"

"All right. Drive around the block and we will cut him off at the other side."

* *

"Yvonne was there, in Thuong Duc, during the war?" asked Jim.

"Yes, she was born in France in 1955, but spent a lot of her childhood in Thuong Duc. It's all in her official papers. I saw it when my men were preparing her travel permit. She has been there many times," said the captain.

"You must be mistaken. She is French and Chinese. She was born in France, she told me so," said a surprised Summerpot.

"True, she was born there, but it's her father who is half French and Chinese.

Yvonne's mother was Vietnamese. In fact, when Dr. Braden fought his last battle in Thuong Duc, Yvonne was a twelve-year-old and she was there. Her grandmother lives there still," said Captain Minh.

Summerpot was in deep thought and Jim was in disbelief.

"You don't say," said Summerpot.

Just then Yvonne entered the room.

"You don't say what? Have I missed something?" asked Yvonne.

Jim looked up, startled, and Captain Minh started to answer, but Summerpot grabbed his sleeve to stop him and spoke instead.

"Ah! My dear. Captain Minh was just commenting on your extraordinary beauty. Please sit down."

Summerpot smiled while he stood to help Yvonne with her chair. Jim and Tran Minh looked confused, but said nothing more, respecting the old fat man's obvious wish not to let Yvonne know they had been talking about her past.

"No, thank you, I'd like to stay, but it is getting late. Please excuse me. I think I'll return to the hotel now," said Yvonne.

“Oh, must you?” asked Madam Lee. “You’ve been such lovely company, my dear. Won’t you reconsider?”

“No, I must really get going,” replied Yvonne.

Captain Minh wanted to escort Yvonne back to the hotel and started to stand and speak, but once again Mr. Summerpot stopped him with a touch to the arm and a queer look.

“Perhaps Dr. Braden could see you back to the hotel. These are dangerous streets for a woman alone,” said Summerpot.

“It’s not necessary,” returned Yvonne.

Jim got up quickly. He wasn’t expecting the fat man to make the suggestion, but was glad he did. He wanted nothing better than to spend more time with Yvonne, and the less people the better.

“It’s no problem. I was losing anyway,’ said Jim.

“Well, If you don’t mind,” said Yvonne.

“Of course not,” Jim replied. “Mr. Summerpot, would you like one of the cabbies to wait for you, too?”

“No, my boy. I prefer Captain Minh’s car. He can drop me off later.”

“Okay then, we’ll see you later. Madam Lee thanks for a lovely evening,” Jim said.

"Yes, thank you so much," added Yvonne.

"My pleasure," replied Madam Lee.

"Summerpot, Captain Minh," said Jim, as he shook their hands goodbye.

Yvonne and Jim turned to leave and an annoyed Captain Minh was beside himself.

"They make a good couple," commented Madam Lee.

"Yes, they do," added Captain Minh. "And, Mr. Summerpot, my fat friend, you'd better have a good reason for keeping me here. I had notions of seeing her home myself."

"Sorry to interfere with your romantic interludes, but there is something I need to see back at your office. You may find it intriguing."

* *

Yvonne's messenger, the man with the crooked nose, was walking briskly down one of the dark city streets leading away from Madam Lee's club. He saw a parked car ahead and crossed the street. The lights came on the car, and it rolled slowly toward him. The messenger stopped and so did the car. Two men got out and headed his way. He turned into an alley directly in front of him. As he rounded the corner he was grabbed. An unseen assailant plunged a knife deep into his chest. The messenger gasped and his body collapsed. The two thugs, from the car, ran into the alley.

Chi Woo, smiling, appeared from behind the wall of the stone building, bent over the body and wiped his knife blade on the dead man's coat.

"Search him," ordered Chi Woo, and the two thugs ripped into the dead messenger's pockets. They found the note and handed it to Chi Woo who read it. Chi Woo smiled again and folded the note up and motioned for the two henchmen to follow him back to the car.

* *

Yvonne and Jim walked outside to the waiting cab squad. The men were playing a gambling game of their own and snapped to their feet when they saw Jim. Cao rushed over to Jim and Yvonne.

"Boss, you go now?" asked Cao.

"Yes, back to the hotel. Tell the men they don't need to wait for Summerpot, he'll be returning later with Captain Minh," said Jim.

Cao yelled the order in Vietnamese and then helped Yvonne into one of the cabs. Jim got into Cao's cab and as they started out, Cao and Jim were bringing up the rear. Jim leaned forward and yelled at the peddling Cao.

"Hey, catch up to her."

"Okay, boss."

Cao nodded and put on more speed. The cabs pulled abreast of one another as they turned on to a busier street with festive nightlife. Jim turned to Yvonne in the next cab.

"Excuse me, Miss Chin. Could I interest you in a nightcap at the hotel bar?"

Yvonne looked confused not hearing that term before.

"Pardon me, a nightcap?" Yvonne said.

"A drink! A glass of wine or something," answered Jim.

"Oh! No, not tonight. Perhaps another time," said Yvonne.

At that moment a car pulled out from the curb cutting off the pedi-cabs and blocking the road, making the squad put on the brakes just in time. Cao was beside himself and jumped off the bike yelling at the car.

"What your problem?"

The two henchmen got out brandishing their automatic pistols. The street people started yelling and running off. Cao was undaunted. Jim was surprised, then afraid for Yvonne, and tried humor as a nervous response to danger.

"Gentlemen, is there a problem?" he asked from the cab seat.

The first henchman raised his handgun and shoved Cao back. Cao smiled.

"We're not afraid of your guns," he said, not taking his eyes off the first henchman.

The cab squad dismounted slowly, but deliberately, and took up positions around Cao and the henchmen. Yvonne was taking it all in and stood up in the pedi-cab. She looked frightened and concerned. Jim stood up himself.

"Cao, I think I better do the talking. Listen gentlemen. Do you speak English? I'm an American and we don't want any…"

"Shut up! And sit down," shouted the first thug. "No one cares who you are or what you want."

Jim was taken back and looked surprised. He hesitated and said nothing more.

The back door of the car slowly opened and Chi Woo got out.

"I should have known," Jim said as he recognized the Chinese gangster.

Chi Woo fussed with his lapel and hat and when he was satisfied with his appearance he approached a few steps.

"Miss Chin, Dr. Braden. How nice to see you once again."

Yvonne looked shocked.

"I'm afraid Miss Chin, I must insist that you come with me. The rest of you may go. We want no trouble," continued Chi Woo.

He pulled out the note Yvonne had given the messenger earlier and unfolded it for her to see. Yvonne looked at it with no emotion. Jim, upset, was not sure what to do, but he couldn't stand by and let them take Yvonne.

"Where's the man who had this note?" asked Yvonne.

"He is no longer with us. Now come with me!" ordered Chi Woo.

"She's not going anywhere, friend. Let's just put away the guns and discuss this like rational human beings," Jim said.

"Dr. Braden, I am beginning to tire of you. No one is going to discuss anything."

Yvonne had not taken her eyes off Chi Woo.

"You're right! And I've become tired of you," screamed Yvonne, as she pulled a semi-automatic pistol out from under her coat and started firing rapidly at Chi Woo.

Chi Woo screamed in pain as he was hit in the arm and leg. The henchmen were so taken by surprise that the cab squad was able to take advantage of their hesitation and jump in to disarm them. Chi Woo scrambled back to the car door bleeding and screaming at the two thugs.

Yvonne had run out of bullets, and Cao jumped on the cab she was standing in and started to peddle away. The force of his peddling knocked Yvonne back into the seat, and Jim jumped out of his cab and followed on the run.

"Boss, come on, hop in," yelled Cao.

As Jim ran faster to catch up, the rest of the cab squad took the two handguns and jumped on the four pedi-cabs disappearing in different directions.

Cao turned right onto a busy street slowing down to make the turn, giving Jim the opportunity to catch up and jump in the cab seat, falling against Yvonne with his head in her lap. Smelling the wonderful scent of her perfume on her raised skirt, he turned his head up and smiled.

"Never a dull moment, Chin!" Jim exclaimed.

Yvonne looked down at him. "No one asked you to get involved, Braden."

Jim righted himself and grabbed her hand in his, and she let him. He laughed at her.

"Well, I'm involved up to my neck now."

Cao peddled faster and soon turned into one alley and then another as he made good their get-away.

Back at the car, Chi Woo was screaming at the two thugs to get him to a hospital. They tried to stop the bleeding with rags ripped from their shirts and finally drove off.

Soon Jim and Yvonne found themselves in a quiet dark alley with Cao peddling steadily, but slower. He pulled into a ramshackle garage type structure with a canvas cover for a door and corrugated tin for a roof. They were quiet as they got out of the cab and went into a straw hut adjacent to the garage.

Cao struck a match and lit a candle. The dim light exposed a rustic thatched room.

There were sleeping mats, three old chairs, some blankets and pillows. One old military metal water can sat in the corner.

"Is this where you live?" asked Jim.

"Yes, this where squad sleeps, but they will be waiting at a place on the Han River for me. It is where we go when we have trouble," answered Cao.

"When are you taking us back to the hotel?" Jim continued.

"Maybe we should wait awhile," said Cao.

"No, we won't be going back," Yvonne said. "Tonight they killed one of my father's trusted men from Thuong Duc, and they will kill you two as well."

"Thuong Duc?" said Cao. "I know that village. Now I remember man with crooked nose, he's from that village. I saw him leave gambling club tonight."

"Yes, I believe they killed him, and now they know my father is in that village, too," said Yvonne.

"Well, Chi Woo won't be going anywhere soon," said Jim. "You hit him in the leg at least once, and by the way, since you brought it up, just what the hell is going on with these men and your father?"

Yvonne ignored Jim and turned back to Cao.

"Cao! Do you think you can get inside the hotel and get our things without anyone knowing?" said Yvonne.

"Yes, I should be able to do it," answered Cao.

"Good. We have our passports and travel permits, but I need a small brown leather valise. Anything else you can get in the way of clothing will be a bonus."

Yvonne turned to Jim. "What about you? What do you need?"

"What about me? What about you? What the hell is going on here?" asked a frustrated Jim.

"James, darling. Shut up!" ordered Yvonne.

*Darling? She called me darling. Did I just imagine that or was it a slip of the tongue.* No matter, it had its intended effect, and he sat still.

"Cao, we will need a vehicle of some kind as well. And we need a place to stay for the night," said Yvonne.

"I know a woman not far from here who rents a very nice room with its own shower and toilet," said Cao. "Very expensive though, two American dollars per night, but it's clean."

"I feel I can trust you. Here, take this money." She handed Cao most of the cash she had in her purse. "Find out if the room's available and get right back here. Then see about a car."

"Yes, maam will do," said Cao.

"What do you mean, yes maam? I thought I was the boss here," said Jim.

"You the boss, boss, but she in charge! Be back soon. Not to worry," said Cao.

"I must be going insane. I meet a beautiful woman, fall in love, I don't know why, and she turns out to be some kind of an Asian *Bonnie and Clyde*," said Jim.

"Here, will this make you feel better?" Yvonne took Jim's face in both of her soft hands and kissed him.

* *

Captain Minh and Summerpot were just leaving Madam Lee's as a smaller police car, with blue lights flashing, pulled up in front of Captain Minh's car. The driver got out quickly, stopping the captain on the sidewalk.

"Sir, sorry to bother you, but there's been a reported shooting not far from here," said the officer.

"Anyone hurt?" asked the captain.

"Yes, I think so, sir. There are bloodstains on the pavement. We have many eye witness reports of a car pulling out in front of a bunch of pedi-cabs forcing them to stop, and then a lot of random gunfire," continued the officer.

Captain Minh and Summerpot gave each other a look of shock.

"Jim and Yvonne," said Summerpot, in a tone of horror.

"Was anyone in the cabs shot?" asked the captain.

"Why, no sir. A woman in one of the cabs did the shooting," returned the officer.

"What!" said the captain and Summerpot simultaneously.

"The woman in the cab did the shooting and at least one of the car occupants was wounded. We have not found the car yet," said the officer.

Summerpot and Captain Minh looked at each other in disbelief.

"All right, show me where this happened. Come on, Mr. Summerpot," said Captain Minh.

"Oh, captain. There is one other thing. A dead man, stabbed in the chest not far from here," said the officer.

"A white man?" asked the captain.

"No, a Vietnamese," answered the officer.

"Okay, let's get moving," said the captain.

The two police cars took off with blue lights flashing and took only a few minutes to reach the scene. Captain Minh got out and started checking the area. The officers sealed off the area, and the captain and Summerpot were quickly shown the bloodstains and empty shell casings.

"Thirty-eight, or nine millimeter caliber casings," said the captain as he picked one of the casings off the ground. "Eight of them all together. Probably a nine millimeter semi-automatic hand gun."

The captain knelt and looked around the scene in deep thought.

"Were the occupants of the auto armed?" asked Summerpot.

The officer waited until he made eye contact with Captain Minh. The captain nodded.

"Yes, sir. The witnesses said they pulled their hand guns first," said the officer.

“But the cab drivers attacked them and stole their guns. The shooter fled in one of the cabs. And the other cabs went in different directions.”

Captain Minh got up looking at Summerpot and chuckling to himself.

“Mr. Summerpot. First I’ll have my driver take you to the Green Plaza Hotel. Check and see if Dr. Braden and Miss Chin are there,” said the captain. “I’ll go and see about this stabbing and then meet you at the hospital. I think we may find someone there we might want to talk to.”

*  *

Cao Vien thanked the woman and told her the guests would be arriving shortly. He walked quickly, taking the alleys and narrower streets until he returned to Jim and Yvonne.

“Someone’s coming,” Yvonne said, as she pulled her Kruger nine millimeter back out of her purse.

“Boss, it’s Cao. I’m coming in,’ said Cao.

“Good, it’s Cao. You can put that thing away now,” said Jim.

"I don't have any more bullets anyway. They're at the hotel," said Yvonne.

Cao came through the canvas door and had Jim and Yvonne follow him back out. They wound their way back to the boarding house, staying in the darkness as much as possible. Jim held Yvonne's hand the whole time. His mind was racing trying to make sense of all that had happened since he left Seattle. He knew one thing for sure. He couldn't live without this woman. Holding her hand sent shock waves up his arms like he hadn't felt with anyone else.

"Here it is," Cao said, as he led the other two back from the street past a green patch of grass.

The two-story cement house had one dim light in the window and two steps up to the porch. An old Vietnamese lady with a toothless grin beckoned them in.

"I will leave you two now. I have to meet with the squad at the river. They will be worried. The old woman has already been paid," said Cao.

"Here's my hotel key," said Yvonne. "James, give him your key."

They handed the keys to Cao.

"Be back in the morning," said Jim.

“It will take time to acquire a car and get your things,” replied Cao. “It might be more like noon.”

“Okay, go!” said Jim.

*  *

Summerpot had the door to Captain Minh’s auto open before the driver came to a stop. For all his size he sprang from the back seat of the car and hurried into the hotel lobby, stopping at the main desk. The same clerk that had dealt with Chi Woo was still on duty.

“Have Dr. Braden and Miss Chin returned this evening?” asked Summerpot.

“No sir,” was the clerk’s reply.

“Are you sure?”

“Yes sir, very sure. Another man, China man I think, was here earlier looking for Miss Chin. He wasn’t a nice man.”

“Miss Chin? Not Dr. Braden?”

“Yes, Miss Chin! He even made me open her room.”

“Chi Woo,” said Summerpot to himself. “But why Miss Chin?”

“Mr. Summerpot, is the police captain with you?” asked the clerk. “I see the blue lights flashing from his car outside.”

"No, my boy. He's not with me."

"Well, would you let him know about the China man?" said the clerk.

"By all means, my son. By all means!"

Summerpot hurried back to the car and it wasn't long before he was sitting in front of the hospital waiting for Captain Minh.

"I say, driver. Do turn those blue lights off would you please. I don't want them to alert anyone inside seeking medical attention," said Summerpot.

The driver complied and the captain arrived soon after, turning the blue lights off in the second police car as well. Summerpot and the captain got out of their cars and met on the sidewalk.

"So, what is the news of Dr. Braden and Miss Chin?" asked Tran Minh.

"They have not returned to the hotel, and there's something else. A man I know, a gangster from Bangkok, shall we say, was looking for Miss Chin at the hotel earlier," said Summerpot. "This man is named Chi Woo and he works for a powerful drug lord. I have dealt with Mr. Woo in the past when it made sense financially, and if Miss Chin is mixed up with him there has to be trouble afoot."

"Drugs!" said Captain Minh. "Summerpot you know I will look the other way with gambling, small extortions and smuggling refugees, but drugs I won't stand for."

"I don't think the girl is mixed up in drugs with this man," said Summerpot. "It must be something else. You must bear with me on this."

"You sound like you are about ready to ask me a favor, my old friend," said Captain Minh.

"You know me too well," returned Summerpot. "I've taken a liking to Dr. Braden and Miss Chin in particular, and when we return to your office and have a look at Miss Chin's file you will understand more. I don't know what the trouble is, but I feel I must help."

"What do you propose?" said the captain.

"I believe that if Miss Chin did in fact shoot someone, it would have to be Chi Woo. Let us make contact with him either here at the hospital or later. I should be able to get him to confide in me."

* *

The rain beat down heavily on the waterfront building and splattered against the one window in Kai-Ling's office. It afforded no additional light in the already dim room. The drug lord was in a foul mood as his plans continued to be blocked by events he could not seem to control, and he was used to controlling everything. A man sat in the shadows, his face hidden from view and only his brass buckled shoes reflecting the faint light.

"I must find Dr. Chin and retrieve that process. There are billions of dollars at risk. And now the girl has fled as well," said Kai-Ling.

"Perhaps it's time you let me handle things personally. We know that they were going to the village of Thuong Duc. At least that idiot Woo gave us that much before he made a mess of things. I'm familiar with that place, and no one knows me there. If the girl and her father are there, I will find them and bring them back."

"If you succeed my friend, I will make you a very important and very rich man."

* *

The old Vietnamese woman led Yvonne and Jim up the second story stairway. She pulled on a string, hanging from the ceiling, and a dim light came on. She opened the door and as she twisted the light switch to the right, a brighter light illuminated the room. There was a fairly big window with no curtain so the city lights shone through. Yvonne was surprised at its cleanliness and although the bathroom only had cold water, it came from a tank on the roof, heated by the sun, and was quite pleasant to touch. The toilet was tolerable and the bathroom door had a lock. The shower was small and the curtain old. Jim thought Mr. Summerpot would not fit in this shower.

The bed wasn't a twin size and wasn't a double either. It had two pillows, and was clean with fresh sheets and pillowcases. It looked like the women had just placed them before they got there.

"Thank you, this will do," said Yvonne in Vietnamese.

Jim, not sure if he would be sleeping on the floor, stopped the woman.

"Do you have some extra blankets?" he asked.

The woman didn't understand and looked to Yvonne.

Speaking in Vietnamese Yvonne told her that he had thanked her and that all was fine. She turned and left and Yvonne closed the door, locking it and then she switched off the light, letting the glow from DaNang light the room. Jim didn't understand what she told the old woman, but he was beginning to feel that he didn't need the extra blankets.

Yvonne stood still in the faint light and said nothing. A million thoughts were going through Jim's mind at once. She was beautiful, she kissed him earlier. And he knew she liked him. He wasn't sure what to do, but he knew he wanted her. He wanted her more than any woman he had ever met. He was afraid at the same time and didn't want to do anything that would turn her away. He took a step toward her.

"James, wait." Yvonne lifted her hand to stop him. "I admit that we have an attraction. It's just that my life is upside down right now. I don't know what will happen from day to day. You've seen my desperation in the fact that I shot a man tonight. I have never done anything like that before."

Jim heard her voice crack and in the light from the window could see tears starting to flow down her cheeks.

"I'm afraid for my father, and I'm afraid for myself. Now I am afraid for you. I don't know what is going to happen next, but I know I'm glad you are with me. Whatever happens between us tonight happens knowing that I can give you no guarantees. Our lives are so different."

Yvonne put her hand down and stood silent. Jim wanted to hold her so badly. He stepped next to her and took her left hand in his right. He looked deeply into her dark eyes. His left hand took her other hand, and he felt her warmth radiate up his arms. He lifted her hands and arms up chest high and pulled her gently toward him. They dropped hands and embraced in a hug and kiss.

* *

# Chapter 7

Captain Minh and Mr. Summerpot entered the hospital and walked to the emergency admitting desk. The other police officer went with them while Captain Minh's driver stayed outside with the cars. Captain Minh flashed his badge to the nurse on duty and spoke in Vietnamese.

"I'm looking for a man with a gunshot wound," said Captain Minh.

The nurse hesitated and looked at both men and then turned around looking at the emergency room door. Captain Minh was impatient.

"Did you hear what I said?" exclaimed Captain Minh, in a demanding tone.

The nurse was quite nervous and finally spoke.

"Yes, captain. He's Chinese and he threatened the doctor and paid lots of cash in return for silence," said the nervous nurse.

"Where is he?"

"In the back room."

Summerpot and the officer followed Captain Minh through the door and into the emergency area. The two Vietnamese thugs were waiting outside the last treatment room and recognized the captain. He recognized them, too. They moved hastily out of the way and let the captain pass.

"Don't you two go anywhere," said Captain Minh.

A yell of pain came from the room and the sound of swearing in Chinese, and then in Vietnamese followed as Chi Woo was chastising the doctor.

"You stupid idiot," cried Chi Woo. "Can't you see I'm still in pain? Get some more pain killer in my leg."

He took a swing at the doctor's head, but missed just as Captain Minh entered the room.

"Doctor," called Captain Minh, in a loud voice. "Leave us."

"Who the hell are you?" asked Chi Woo. "I'm still bleeding."

Captain Minh looked at Chi Woo's bleeding leg and arm and then at the gangster. He flashed his badge.

"I'm Captain Minh, DaNang police. Who shot you and why?"

Chi Woo didn't answer, looking straight ahead. Then he noticed Mr. Summerpot and gave a look of surprised recognition.

"I asked you a question," continued an upset Captain Minh.

"You are nobody to be asking me questions," said a defiant Chi Woo.

Captain Minh was enraged; the thought of this drug dealer talking to him in that way made his blood boil. He hated drug dealers and wanted to shoot the Chinese thug himself, but Summerpot took his arm in a calming gesture and spoke first.

"Captain Minh, my friend," said Summerpot. "I know this man, and I can vouch for him. He has high connections in your government."

Captain Minh had more than an instant dislike for Chi Woo, but he was going to let Summerpot play his hand. He stared intently at Chi Woo, but backed off.

"Mr. Woo, Captain Minh is a person that your associates would like to know and have as a friend when in DaNang," continued Summerpot, with a look at Chi Woo that said, play along with me.

Chi Woo's scowl turned to a smirk.

"I'm sorry," smiled Chi Woo. "I forgot my manners. Of course, Captain Minh, I apologize. I have been shot and I'm in pain. Please forgive me."

"I'll have the doctor come back in," said the captain, with a stern look still etched on his face.

"Good," said Summerpot.

* *

The light from the DaNang skyline shone through the large window highlighting the faces of Jim and Yvonne. He held her tightly with one arm while softly stroking her long black hair with the other.

"I didn't want you coming to Vietnam," said Yvonne. "Of all places, you were asking about Thuong Duc, my village. I thought you were working with Chi Woo since you kept popping up everywhere I was."

"Let me get this straight. It was you who set up the shooting in Bangkok?" said Jim.

"I had no choice. My father's life was in danger. I had to scare you off," answered Yvonne.

Jim shifted his body on the bed so he could look at her better. The scent of her perfume was intense and the flame from making love to her was still burning fresh in his mind, but it was time to get the facts out.

"Okay. Tell me what is going on and why Thuong Duc is so important," said Jim.

Yvonne took a deep breath and sighed. She looked at Jim and kissed him on the cheek.

"My father is a chemist, a brilliant man. He is the son of a prominent Chinese Lord and a colonial French girl from Hanoi. My grandparents, both are dead. My father had been working for years with native plants that had medicinal value with the hope of turning common plants into high-grade medicines. Inexpensive medicines and products that would have given developing Asian nations access to more modern healthcare, without relying on expensive drugs from the west. In his research he stumbled across a process that would change mountain poppies into the purest of heroine derivatives at one-tenth the current cost. One of my father's assistants saw the value in this and went to the Thai Drug Lords. They secretly funded my father's work, without his knowledge, through third parties, while making plans to flood the western markets with inexpensive heroine."

"So what happened?" asked Jim.

"My father got wind of it and destroyed all his research. He burned his lab and fled," answered Yvonne.

"But I still don't see what this has to do with me. Why were you so bent on making me return home," said Jim.

"Because of Thuong Duc!" said Yvonne. "My father was educated in Paris and returned to Hanoi in 1954 just prior to the defeat of the French at Dien Bien Phu. The communists killed my father's parents, but my father escaped to South Vietnam. DaNang first, and then Thuong Duc."

"Almost forty years ago. He must have met your mother there," said Jim.

"Yes, you're right. My mother was born there. She was only sixteen when my father met her, but they were attracted to one another right away. They soon fell in love, but life was hard for them. Their match was not accepted, and as soon as my father received the money his parents left him, he took her away, and eventually went to France."

"What do you mean, they weren't accepted," asked Jim.

"My father wasn't Vietnamese," said Yvonne. "The villagers did not accept him. They didn't like mixed marriages, and they were already tolerant of my grandmother because my mother's father was not Vietnamese. That is probably why my father was so faithful all those years sending money to my grandmother."

"Your grandmother? Why?"

"When he took my mother away it broke my grandmother's heart. She was an only child. The money my father sent allowed my grandmother to live a good life and since she shared her good fortune she gained a high status. My grandmother would not talk of my grandfather, but I always assumed he was French."

"How did you end up living there?" Jim asked.

"How did you know I lived there?" asked Yvonne in return.

"Captain Minh. He knows all about you. He has a file," said Jim.

"I see … Yes, I spent my adolescent years in Thuong Duc. When I was almost seven, my mother wanted to go back and see my grandmother, and take me. The war with the north had not escalated yet, but my father knew it would soon. The plan was to be gone a month. My father was going to be in Bangkok working, so my mother and I went to Vietnam alone. My mother never returned."

Yvonne paused and just stared into the darkness. Jim looked at her lovingly. He kissed her cheek and held her tighter. Yvonne thought of the little girl earlier in the evening. She was that girl years ago, lost, without her mother.

"Do you want to tell me what happened to her?" said Jim.

She took Jim's hand and held it tightly.

"She was killed by the North Vietnamese. They came to the village looking for food, just days before we were to leave. She had a French passport. My grandmother hid me in a hole in the ground under her bed," said Yvonne as tears streamed down her cheeks.

"Yvonne, I'm so sorry," said Jim.

Jim held her tighter for a moment then Yvonne pulled away and straightened herself upright.

"It took my father almost eight years to get me back. He couldn't come to Vietnam with the war escalating so he found ways to send money. My grandmother, once again, shared it with everyone. It helped the village stand up against the North and survive the war. Now those people who hated my father for not being Vietnamese would do anything for him."

"I still don't see why I was such a threat to him," said Jim.

"We were seen together getting on the same plane in Seattle. We were seen together in Bangkok. You came to my store. Whether we were or not it seemed that we were connected in their eyes," said Yvonne. "My father is hiding near Thuong Duc. You would have led them to him."

"I get it. They would have followed me here. I see it now," said Jim. "And your father, is he there now?"

"Yes. I sent a man to warn him, but Chi Woo killed him. That is why I shot him," said Yvonne.

"And what about Chi Woo?" asked Jim.

"He works for the drug lords. He tried to offer me money and persuade me to make my father reveal his process. I strung him along for a while," said Yvonne. "Now he is playing a more serious game. None of us are safe now. I'm sorry."

"Well, they haven't got us yet. What's your plan now?" asked Jim.

"That depends on your ex-ranger friends and how trustworthy they are," said Yvonne. "I must warn my father as soon as possible. Chi Woo knows about Thuong Duc now."

* *

Chi Woo was sitting in a wheelchair, in the hospital waiting room, with his bandaged left leg raised horizontal to the floor; his left arm in a sling. Summerpot was sitting next to him waiting for the doctor to return with a prescription of pain pills. One of the Vietnamese thugs stood at the back of the chair.

"So, Mr. Woo, what is your interest in Miss Chin?" asked Summerpot.

"I might ask you the same. You flew here with her and Dr. Braden," said Chi Woo.

"Quite by accident I assure you, Mr. Woo," returned Summerpot. "At first I thought your attention was directed at Dr. Braden when I saw you drive by after that unfortunate shooting in front of the Vietnamese Embassy."

"He was my attention, … then. I had no part in that shooting. He would be dead if I had been."

"So, again, what is your involvement with the girl?" asked the fat man.

"It's none of your business," said Chi Woo.

"On the contrary, I feel I could be of some assistance to you. There has been a lot of talk about a village called Thuong Duc. A village I know very well," said Summerpot.

Chi Woo was noticeably shocked at the mention of Thuong Duc and Summerpot smiled at him.

"I see I've touched a nerve," continued Summerpot.

"What do you want?" asked Chi Woo.

"Just a chance to make a piece of whatever action is going down here. My bank account has been diminishing of late," said the fat man. "And I did convince Captain Minh to look the other way on your behalf."

Chi Woo looked closely at Summerpot as the doctor returned with the pain pills and handed them to the gangster, leaving swiftly without a word.

"My car is outside. Maybe you can be of service. Let's go."

The Vietnamese thug wheeled Chi Woo out the open door with Summerpot following.

*　*

Cao Vien peddled his cab back to the rental yard where all the other cabs had been parked for some time. He looked around and headed off toward the River Han. A few blocks later he ducked into a small cafe and left by a back door. Certain that no one had followed him he hurriedly found the cab squad hiding along an old pier on the west side of the Han River. His friends were glad to see him, and he told them of Yvonne's request.

"We have two options as I see it," Cao explained. "We can take this money, and these two guns, and disappear and eat well for a long while, or we can do as she asked and maybe something better will come of it."

The squad thought it over, and each man said his piece pro and con. Finally Cao spoke again.

"We have had a hard life my friends. I for one feel something strong about this U. S. Marine and this French woman. No one else is going to give us shit! I want to help them, if nothing else, for the respect they showed us. What do you say?"

The squad agreed and they moved out, one at a time, planning to meet back at their hut and get some much needed sleep. They would hide the two handguns for use later. Cao waited until all the men were gone and proceeded to find a man he knew that had an old French Peugeot automobile.

Cao was once again very careful in his trip across town, keeping to less traveled streets and allies. He found his friends house at the end of a deserted street. Thanh, his friend, had his concrete garage locked tight with a padlock. Cao gently banged on a window of the house. By now it was very early in the morning.

"Thanh, Thanh, you awake. It's Cao," said Cao.

There was no sound for some time, and Cao banged again.

"Who is it?" Thanh's voice came through the closed window. "What do you want?"

"Thanh, its Cao. Cao Vien. I need to talk to you."

"Go away. It's too early to talk. Go beg somewhere else," came Thanh's reply, his face pressing up against the glass.

"I'm not begging," said Cao. "I have money, lots of money."

Cao lifted his bankroll spreading out the bills like a hand of playing cards for his friend to see. Thanh took one look and opened the door.

"Quick. Get inside before someone sees you," said Thanh. "Where did you get that? Did you rob someone?"

"No! You know I would never do that," returned Cao.

"I'm not so sure. What do you want with me?" asked Thanh.

"I need you and your car. I have a rich American man and a beautiful French woman who need a car and driver," said Cao.

"Where are they? Why do they not come? Why do they send you?" asked Thanh.

"They have a bit of trouble with a Chinese man. They need to be very discreet. They will pay well," said Cao. "Does the car run?"

"Does the car run, he asks," said Thanh. "Of course it runs. Come."

Thanh got a set of keys from inside his house and walked the ten feet to the concrete garage. He opened the padlock, and the double wooden doors swung open revealing an old dusty car. The inside of the garage was packed with spare parts and tires making it hard to get inside.

"There it is. My beautiful 1948 Peugeot 203," said Thanh.

Cao looked at the old car and thought beautiful was stretching it a bit. The old Peugeot was a faded blue color with rusty chrome grill and bumpers. The single front window was topped with a metal visor to keep the sun out and there was only one windshield wiper on the driver's side. The left front headlight was missing, as were all the hubcaps. It was a four-door sedan with the front doors in the suicide position opening out into the wind. The interior was a dirty brown cloth fabric, but without any major holes or damage.

"Will it run?" asked Cao again.

"Yes!" Thanh sounded offended, but Cao ignored him.

"Out to Thuong Duc," said Cao.

"Where?" asked Thanh.

"Thuong Duc. It's about thirty-five kilometers southwest of here in the mountains," said Cao. "Along the Song Vu

Gia River. I was stationed there during the war."

"I will need a full tank of petrol and some extra motor oil," said Thanh.

"They can pay, but first we need to go to the Green Plaza Hotel and get their baggage. I have the keys to their rooms."

"When do you want to go?" asked Thanh.

"At daylight. It would arouse too much suspicion to do it now. I will sleep in the car and wake you at first light," said Cao. "Here is a down payment."

He handed Thanh a few bills, and got inside the Peugeot. Thanh took the money and went inside his house leaving the garage doors open.

* *

Jim grabbed the blanket and pulled it over his head. The sun was breaking over the South China Sea and the first rays of sunlight were streaking in the window. He momentarily forgot where he was and looked around the lackluster room in panic. A noise from the bathroom, water trickling, helped bring him back to reality. She was still here; he hadn't dreamed it. He lay there trying to think about all that had happened the last three days. It was bittersweet. He was in love once again. It was a whirlwind of intrigue and desperation. He wished he could take her away and get on a plane to safety, but he knew she had a mission and a responsibility to her father. He was unaware of the danger lurking close by.

Jim sat up on the bed and looked out the window at the city of DaNang. It looked so different now. Gone were all the Marines and their heavy equipment, replaced by motor scooters and bicycles. Already the city was awake and busy. The streets were filling up with people going to work or the market. He saw the old landlady sweeping the walkway to the street. He wished he had his bags and his toothbrush.

* *

Cao Vien was awake at the first sound of morning. He got out of the Peugeot and crept over to the house door. This time he banged loudly. Thanh was already up and dressing, as he was excited about the possibility of making money. He had a pot of tea on the wood burning stove and greeted Cao with a cup when he opened the door.

"Come in my friend," said Thanh. "Drink this tea and then we will start the car. The battery should be good. I charge it every week with an old American battery charger I bought."

"When does the petrol station open?" asked Cao.

"It's open now, we'll go there first."

"After we fuel the car we need to pick up my men," said Cao.

"Those dirty, ragged fellows, in my beautiful car," replied Thanh.

"They're not ragged any more. See my new clothes. They all have the same new clothes now," said Cao. "Look, I need them to help get the baggage from the hotel. They are good men. They have helped you when you were in need, have they not?"

"Okay, Okay! They better not tear the seats. Come on, finish your tea and let's get going," said Thanh.

The two men gulped down the remainder of their tea and moved outside. Thanh locked the house door and went over to the Peugeot. He bent over, felt for the hood release and popped the hood. The old blue paint was faded and a chip fell away as the rusty springs squeaked as if begging for a drink of oil.

Thanh set to work connecting the battery cables as Cao watched. He had never been around automobiles much and wished he had the skills to be a mechanic. Even ex-rangers that could fix motors had good jobs.

"There, that should do it," exclaimed Thanh.

He moved around the driver's side of the car and opened the suicide door. Grabbing the steering wheel he ducked inside and made himself comfortable. Putting in the clutch, he found neutral and after pumping the gas pedal twice and pulling out the choke, he turned the key. As old as it was, the Peugeot 203 came to life, all four cylinders humming away without missing a beat. Thanh was all smiles.

"Get in, let's get your men," said Thanh.

Cao got in the front passenger door and Thanh put the car in gear. They slowly pulled out of the garage and went a short distance.

"Oh, could you lock the garage for me?" asked Thanh.

Cao nodded and jumped out leaving the car door open. He quickly closed the doors and locked the padlock. They were soon cruising down the streets past the busy morning traffic of pedestrians, motor scooters and bicycles. Thanh, very proud of his Peugeot, was very lucky to have it.

He was born in Hanoi and had relatives from the North. During the war he had not been political, choosing instead to favor whoever was in charge at the time. When he had lived in Saigon during the time of the Americans, he had been able to use his skills as a motor cab driver and make a good deal of money, saving most of it and always being careful to compliment Northern sympathizers and communists when they happened to be in his presence.

Therefore when the Americans left and he was sure that the North would eventually take over he did the opposite of most South Vietnamese. He hid his money and headed north to DaNang, pretending to be a communist sympathizer. Once he was established in DaNang and the North took over the rest of the country, Thanh used his money to buy the old 1948 Peugeot and turn it into a one-man limousine service. He did well as many wealthy Russian, Chinese and Eastern European vacationers flocked to DaNang's white sand beaches.

One day, years before, Cao and his team of cabbies found Thanh stuck with a dead battery and with the jealousy of the common people toward the fairly well to do Thanh, nobody would help push his car to get it started. Nobody, that is, except Cao and his men. They came to the rescue pushing the car until it started. A thankful Thanh drove them to the pedi-cab rental yard and set them up with jobs. From time to time he would drop off food for the half starved men.

The old blue car pulled into the alley behind the squad's shed and came to a stop. Cao's men heard the car and came out giving Thanh greetings and waves of hello.

"Get in the back, we have work to do," yelled Cao.

Thanh put on the gas and the group headed to the filling station some blocks away. It was only their second time in a car and the squad relished the experience. They soon pulled up to the gas pump and stopped.

"Thanh, are you hungry?" asked Cao.

"Yes, I could stand some breakfast," answered Thanh.

"There's a restaurant stand over there with Gia Lau cooking in a pot," said Cao. "I'll send the men over with a few dong and we'll have some food."

Cao gave the squad a few Dong and they soon were all feasting on the Gia Lau, large bowls of lean pork boiled in banana leaves with Pho noodles. The Peugeot was topped off and the well-fed group drove on to the Han River area a few blocks from the Green Plaza Hotel where they stopped.

"We can't have all you guys that are dressed the same come into the Green Plaza. It would look suspicious," said Thanh. "They know me in there because I have picked up vacationers many times in the past. I will park out back, Cao will come with me, and you four will take the bags and load them in the trunk when we set them outside."

"Okay, sounds good to me," said Cao, as the squad nodded their approval.

* *

The old Vietnamese woman was happy to cook breakfast for her guests and was delighted when Yvonne accepted the invitation. Both Yvonne and Jim were hoping Cao would show up with their baggage, so they could change clothes. At least the old lady's shower had worked albeit on the cold side.

"What are we having for breakfast?" asked Jim.

"Let's see what she has," said Yvonne, as she sat at the dining table and uncovered the breakfast bowl. “Oh, you should like this, James. It’s called Pork Banh Cuon. It’s pork wrapped in thin rolls of rice flour. See, you dip it in this sweet and sour sauce and pop them in your mouth.”

Jim took a roll and dipped it.

“Hey, not bad. A little spicy,” he said, as he went for a cup of tea.

Jim looked at his watch. It was 9:45 a.m.

“What do we do if Cao doesn’t come back?” asked Jim.

“I think our only other option is to try and go back to the hotel and find Mr. Summerpot. He might help us avoid Chi Woo and find us some transportation,” said Yvonne. “You know, James, you don’t have to go with me. In fact, I wish you would leave and go back home. I can write you when all this is over, I promise.”

“Have another Banh Cuon. I’m not leaving.”

*　　*

Captain Minh was indeed surprised at what he and Summerpot had found in Yvonne Chin’s file. He slept restlessly during the night and wasn’t sure he should trust

Summerpot completely. He had his men at the Green Plaza and at the private residence where Chi Woo was recovering. He was just waiting for a call.

He was drinking his after breakfast coffee and thinking about the previous night's events. He was especially thinking about Cao and his cabbies. A smile came to his lips when he thought of five undernourished men in rags disarming the two Chi Woo henchmen. He disliked Chi Woo immensely and had done some checking on him. It was evident that his inquiries were stopped cold, and he was ordered from higher up to forget all about Chi Woo. This irritated captain Minh to no end. He had visions of personal power and an ego to match and at the same time wanted to uphold the law of the land, especially when it didn't interfere with him profiting in some way.

He thought of Cao and the ex-Rangers again. Battle hardened veterans, prison survivors, and men capable of loyalty.

"Perhaps I have underestimated these men," he said to himself.

RING!

Captain Minh picked up his phone. It was his undercover man at the Green Plaza. Cao was there with another man.

"I'll be right there. Sit as close to the front desk as you can so I can find you. Have your other man watch them if they leave. And I won't be wearing my uniform," said the captain.

* *

Cao and Thanh walked into the Green Plaza Hotel lobby and Thanh greeted a bell captain he knew before they headed up the main stairway, avoiding the elevator. Yvonne's room was closest, and they went there first. After seeing no one in the hall, they opened the door and went inside. Cao started filling the two suitcases with clothes from the closet and chest of drawers, while Thanh snatched up the free toiletries and threw them in Yvonne's brown leather valise.

"We need a cart," said Thanh. "Then we can take all of it at once. And I need some money for the bell captain."

Cao gave him some small bills and continued packing. Thanh took the elevator this time and got out at the lobby. He saw his friend and motioned for him.

"Thao, I need a baggage cart," said Thanh as he slipped the bell captain some money. "And I need the use of the utility elevator."

Thao looked back at the desk and grabbed a cart. He motioned Thanh back into the elevator and joined him.

Cao was finished with Yvonne's room when Thao and Thanh rejoined him, and the three men loaded Yvonne's things on the cart. A swift ride to the next floor found them in front of Dr. Braden's room. Unlike Yvonne, Jim had unpacked very little and only had the one suitcase and his carry-on bag. They were out of the room within seconds.

Captain Minh, dressed in plain clothes, wide sunglasses and a crushable hat, found his man at the hotel lobby.

"What's going on?" asked the captain.

"I believe they are taking luggage out of at least one room with the help of the bell captain," said the undercover officer. "Look, here comes my man now."

A second undercover man was walking briskly over to the captain.

"Sir, they are leaving by the utility elevator. There is an old blue Peugeot parked in the loading zone in the alley," reported the second officer.

"Quick, let's get to my car," said Captain Minh.

Cao's men had the car loaded promptly with Jim and Yvonne's baggage as Thanh was starting the car.

"All of you go to work as usual, and if I don't get there in time, take this money and have a good lunch," said Cao as he hopped in the passenger side of the Peugeot.

The squad moved out of the alley in one direction and the Peugeot drove out the other.

Captain Minh and his officers were waiting in his car when the blue sedan turned on to the main street running south along the Han River.

"We have to be discreet," said the captain, "or they will know we are following them."

Captain Minh waited a few seconds and then pulled out into traffic. This was his personal 1990 Kia Capital, and it did not have police markings or a police license. They followed at a distance as the blue Peugeot made its way west to a residential district. When they saw the old sedan stop, Captain Minh had one of the undercover officers get out and walk toward the stopped Peugeot.

Yvonne and Jim went outside as soon as they heard the car motor.

"Cao, you did it," said Jim.

"Cao, I knew we could count on you," added Yvonne, as she hugged the thin man firmly.

"This is Thanh. He is the owner and driver of the car," said Cao.

Jim shook Thanh's hand and Yvonne nodded at him. "James, as much as I would like to change clothes, I feel we must be going right away," she said.

"Yes, the sooner we're out of here the better," said Jim.

Yvonne turned to Thanh and spoke in Vietnamese.

"Do you know the roads going west as far as Dai Loc?" she asked.

"Yes, madam," answered Thanh.

"What is your rate?"

"I usually get twenty-five U.S. dollars a half day for car and driver, which is me!" said Thanh.

"Very good," exclaimed Yvonne. "You may have to spend the night on the road for which I will pay you double, in advance. Is this okay with you?" asked Yvonne.

"Yes, madam," said Thanh. "I can sleep in the car."

"Good!" Yvonne counted out fifty U. S. dollars and Thanh was very pleased. She hurried Jim into the car and said goodbye to Cao.

"Wait, Miss Chin," said Cao. "I still have the rest of this money you gave me last night."

"Keep it my friend, you earned it."

With that the blue Peugeot sped off. Cao turned back and started to walk downtown. He only got a half a block when he noticed the undercover officer get into a white Kia in front of him. He didn't make eye contact as he walked by, but out of the corner of his eye he saw the window roll down.

"Sergeant Vien!" the voice called.

Cao stopped and took a deep breath.

"Sergeant Vien, please, come over here," said Captain Minh.

Cao turned and every nerve in his body tensed as visions of prison and torture re-entered his mind. He walked to the car and recognized Captain Minh.

"Get in," said the captain.

*   *

# Chapter 8

The old blue Peugeot was quite comfortable, and Yvonne and Jim were enjoying the ride. They had left the confines of DaNang and were driving southwest on the main dirt road blowing clouds of red dust as they went. Picturesque rice paddies and thatched roofed villages spread before them. Green hills with tropical broadleaf trees and Asian pine rose above the slow moving muddy rivers. *Nothing much has changed in twenty-five years*, thought Jim, as he watched a farmer guide his water buffalo along a flooded rice paddy.

Thanh couldn't drive very fast because of the poor condition of the road and the many pedestrians and scooters that were always in front of them. And children were everywhere. Jim could not believe how many children he saw along their path. It seemed that more than half the population was less than fifteen years old.

They drove past an ancient Cham temple made of red stone with many head of brown cattle grazing on the luxuriant green grass in the courtyard. A water wheel lifting water from an irrigation canal into a rice paddy, manned by a lone farmer, was passed as the blue sedan made its way west. Soon the car was topping a rise on a broad green wooded hill and heading down the western side toward a river crossing.

The Peugeot passed a man on a bicycle, one of a thousand they had passed that morning, but this man stopped and watched the old blue sedan intently as it drove away. He continued after it at renewed speed.

At the bottom of the hill before the bridge was a small village with a market and two small roadside restaurants. Jim also noticed a police checkpoint with a red barrier and two young policemen with AK-47 rifles checking those vehicles heading west over the bridge.

"Hey, I think I recognize this river crossing. I may have been here before," said Jim.

"Thanh," said Yvonne, "there is a police checkpoint up ahead. Let me do the talking. When they let us through, stop before going on the bridge so we can get some bottled water and fresh fruit for lunch."

"Yes, madam," said Thanh.

A truck and a few motor scooters were ahead of them when they came to a stop, and Jim noticed that one guard was checking the vehicles and the other was waving through the pedestrians and bicycles without paying them any attention. *Must be locals*, he thought.

The older man on the bicycle had caught them now and slowed briefly as he peddled by. He looked attentively at Jim and Yvonne and then, without missing a beat, he was waved through the checkpoint and sped down the bridge with great alacrity.

Thanh pulled the Peugeot ahead and the young guard, seeing foreigners in the car, took extra care, eyeing it suspiciously. He walked around the car with his shouldered AK-47 and stopped at Thanh's window.

"Do you own the car?" said the guard.

"Yes," said Thanh.

He already had his tourist permit out and handed it to the guard. The guard looked it over and stared at Jim and Yvonne. This gave Jim the creeps because this police guard was not dressed like the ones in DaNang. He was dressed in the green and red North Vietnamese uniform with the same green pith helmet the NVA wore years ago during the war. He looked closely at the banana shaped magazine inserted the loaded way into the AK-47. The safety was in the fire position.

"This is a little unnerving," said Jim, as he touched Yvonne's arm. She smiled at him with a look of no concern.

The guard handed the permit back to Thanh as Yvonne rolled down her window the rest of the way.

"Who are your passengers?" the guard said to Thanh.

Before he could reply Yvonne spoke in Vietnamese.

"Excuse me, young man," said Yvonne "We have travel permits from DaNang."

The guard was surprised that Yvonne spoke Vietnamese, and as he stepped back toward her, he was obviously taken with her beauty. He hardly noticed Jim and the slight smile broke his lips.

"Good morning, madam," said the young guard politely. "Let me see them please."

Yvonne handed her permit to the guard.

"You are an antiquities dealer. Can I see your passport?" asked the guard.

"Yes, here it is."

"It's a Thai passport, but you were born in France and have dual citizenship," said the guard. "We studied the colonial French occupation in school, but I have never met a French lady before. And the gentleman, he is French also."

"No, he is not. You may be surprised at his passport as well," said Yvonne, with a big smile.

This intrigued the young man, and he asked for Jim's permit and passport.

"James, he wants your permit and passport," said Yvonne.

Jim got his passport and papers out and handed them to the guard who looked them over.

"He is an American," said the guard, not believing his eyes.

"Not only is he an American, but a doctor also, and what's more important, he was a U. S. Marine during the war," replied Yvonne.

This brought a scowl of sorts to the young soldier's face.

"What is his business here?" questioned the guard with a stricter tone.

"This man was wounded twenty-five years ago by the North Vietnamese. He is returning to Thuong Duc village to make his peace. As a policeman you can surely understand this," said Yvonne.

The young policeman was a soldier for two years before joining the police force, had never been in combat, and had never fired his AK-47 except on the practice range. He bent down and looked through the window at Jim as he spoke. Jim smiled at him for lack of not knowing what else to do.

"I have never seen an American before either," said the young policeman. "He looks like a nice man."

"James, show him some of your old pictures with the Thuong Duc kids," said Yvonne.

Jim had his carry-on bag next to him and pulled out a few pictures, handing them to the guard. The guard looked at them and called his companion over and explained who Jim was. Jim in turn pointed at the pictures.

"That's me," he said pointing to the young Marine in the pictures, then pointing back at himself.

The guards smiled and seemed satisfied with the whole encounter. They handed the pictures back to Jim and nodded their approval. The first guard gave the command to pass through, but Yvonne asked if they could park just ahead and visit the market. The guards agreed, and Thanh pulled off the side of the road.

* *

Tran Minh drove the 1990 Kia Capital to police headquarters with Cao Vien in the back seat next to one of the officers. Cao had said nothing the whole way to headquarters, expecting the worst.

"Good work this morning, men. You two can take the rest of the day off," said Captain Minh, to his two undercover officers. "Let them know inside that I will be out for a few hours longer."

"What about him?" asked the first officer, pointing to Cao.

"Yes. What to do with sergeant Vien? Would you join me in the front seat?" said the captain, looking at Cao.

Cao was apprehensive. He didn't figure on events unfolding this way. The undercover officers were surprised, too. Cao cautiously got out of the back door and slid slowly into the front seat of the Kia.

"Men, forget you ever saw this cabby with me, understand!" said Captain Minh, to his undercover officers.

They nodded, turned and walked inside police headquarters.

"Relax, sergeant. I mean you no harm," said Tran Minh. "Are you hungry? I know a small place that serves good food and the owner keeps his mouth quiet about who eats there."

* *

Jim and Yvonne were looking at the fresh produce on display. Beans, rice, bananas, mangoes, corn and other foodstuff was abundant. A steaming pot of rice was simmering next to the produce stand as an old woman with beetle-nut stained teeth stirred it in a smooth rotating motion.

"Mmm, it smells good. "I'll take a bowl," said Yvonne to the old woman.

"I'll stick with bananas," said Jim.

"Come on," said Yvonne. "Take a smell."

She beckoned Jim over and he took a deep sniff and looked in the pot.

"Those are fish heads," Jim sneered. "Gosh, how can you people eat this stuff? Fish heads and rice, I'm going to be sick."

The old woman smiled and got a bowl for Yvonne while Thanh came over. He took a deep sniff of the pot.

"Smells good. I'll take his," laughed Thanh.

* *

The old man on the bicycle had been peddling hard for some time not knowing how soon the dusty blue Peugeot would catch up to him. He was exhausted, but took one look back along the road and then moved off the deserted highway. This far in the country the roads were sparsely populated. He stashed his bicycle in some bushes and covered a short distance up a hill. He climbed rapidly and found a younger man sleeping in the late morning sun.

"Quang, some wealthy foreigners are at the check point. They have a car and driver I have not seen before," said the older man.

The younger man jumped up, fully alert and pulled an old American M-16 from the tall grass. He reversed the magazine and chambered a round before handing it to the older man.

"Quickly then, let's get ready," said the young man.

He grabbed another M-16 out of the tall grass and repeated arming the weapon. The two men moved quickly down the hill to a three-wheeled motor vehicle. It was a Chinese 150cc tricycle truck. The young man threw his M-16 in the rear bed and pulled the little truck's starter cord. On the third try the engine came to life, and the young man drove it out to the main road. He parked it in such a way to block the road and hurriedly jacked the rear axle and removed a rear tire. He gave his M-16 to the older man who threatened a few passersby to hurry them along and then disappeared into the bushes. The young man waited in back of the truck with his eyes glued to the road.

Yvonne and Thanh finished their rice and fish and, along with Jim, got back in the car. They waved goodbye to the young guards and motored off across the bridge.

"How much further do you think it is?" asked Jim.

"We're over half way," said Yvonne. "Not long now."

"Hey, there's the river again and that large sand bar looks familiar," said Jim. "When I first came out here, it was by truck and we were mortared off and on for two days until we reached the Special Forces Camp at Thuong Duc."

The old sedan rounded a bend in the road and Thanh spotted the three-wheeled truck blocking the highway. He was suspicious and slowed way down.

"Truck broke down ahead," said Thanh.

Yvonne and Jim leaned forward and strained to see the scene from the back seat.

"I don't like this," said Thanh. "There are bandits at times in these remote places."

"There is only one young man," said Jim. "Stop a ways back and let him come to us. Yvonne you do the talking, and Thanh be ready to put it in reverse."

Thanh brought the old blue Peugeot to a stop some ways back from the truck. The young thief was concerned, but got up and walked toward the car.

"Sorry to block the road," said Quang in Vietnamese. "My friends should be back soon with the repaired tire."

The three in the car said nothing, and Quang felt uneasy about this situation.

"You might be able to get by. If you want to try I can guide you past. If you land in the ditch it will be hard to get out," said Quang.

"See where that side road leads," said Jim, not knowing that Quang, the thief, spoke and understood a lot of English.

Yvonne spoke to the young man in Vietnamese. "Where does that side road lead to?" she asked.

Quang was no fool and suspected that they would go where he told them not to.

"That road," he said, looking to the side, "it goes south a few hundred meters and then rejoins the main road. It is very rough and bumpy. I think you should try and pass by my truck."

"What do you think, Thanh?" asked Jim.

"I think he wants us to get stuck in the ditch," Thanh replied.

"I think you're right," agreed Jim. "Yvonne, let me see the Kruger. I think he needs to see that we are armed."

Yvonne pulled the empty handgun out of her valise and handed it to Jim.

"Remember, it's out of bullets," she reminded him.

Quang couldn't help but smile inside, but didn't react.

"Not want trouble," said Quang, in a pretense of panic.

"No trouble," said Yvonne. "We are going to try the other road. There may be bandits on such a lonely path so we came prepared."

Quang nodded and turned to walk back to the three-wheeled truck. Thanh put the car in gear and slowly moved out along the side road. They passed some trees a few meters in and turned around the first bend. To their horror the road ended and a large log came crashing down behind the blue Peugeot.

Quang sprinted into the thicket and retrieved his M-16 from the older man who had just pushed over the log. Inside the car they knew they had been had.

"What the hell!" said Jim.

"We're in trouble," said Thanh.

"Shit!" said Yvonne.

Jim got out of the car and raised the empty Kruger.

"James, get back in here," screamed Yvonne.

Quang walked out of the thicket behind the fallen log with his M-16 shouldered. He walked right toward Jim.

“It has no bullets,” the young thief said in English.

Jim looked at the handgun and then back at Quang with his M-16. He realized the kid spoke English. He raised his hands slightly. Quang swung the M-16 around and pointed it at Jim. Thanh sat in his car with the motor still running. Yvonne got out of the car as the older thief made an appearance with his M-16.

“It seems we’re out gunned,” said Yvonne.

“Why did I have to be so greedy,” said Thanh, still sitting in the driver’s seat. “I could be home now taking a nap.”

*  *

# Chapter 9

Summerpot came out of the hotel elevator and crossed over to the clerk at the main desk.

"Excuse me, my good man," said Summerpot. "Have I received any messages this afternoon?"

"Mr. Summerpot. Just the man I came to see," said Captain Minh.

Summerpot turned and saw the captain.

"Never mind," he said to the clerk.

"Come this way my friend. We need to talk."

Summerpot followed Captain Minh to a couch near the window and sat down.

"What news of Dr. Braden and the girl?" asked the fat man.

"They have procured a car and are on their way to Thuong Duc," said Captain Minh, still standing.

"What about this Chinese gangster?" asked Captain Minh.

"Try as I may he won't reveal why he wants the girl, but he has agreed to let me take him there. I have no choice but to go along and see what unfolds," said Summerpot.

"He's going to kill someone, my friend," said the captain. "That man is a killer."

"I still have some influence with his superiors, and if the worst happens, maybe I can help spare the girl," continued Summerpot. "They want something from her, but I can't think of what it might be."

"I have to be careful in dealing with him. I wish I could do more, but there are too many eyes and ears in DaNang," said the captain. "Good luck to you."

*   *

Jim, Yvonne, and Thanh were tied up against a tree with the older thief holding a rifle on them. The younger thief had returned to the three-wheeled truck and was putting the tire back on.

"You know, Yvonne, my sweet. I don't know why I'm surprised. When I fell in love, I had hoped it would be less tension and more compassion," said Jim.

"James, my dear," answered Yvonne. "I blame you for all of this and if we get out of this you will owe me plenty."

"Me? Why?"

"Because you're the man, and the man is always at fault."

"I still like you," returned Jim.

The young thief started the tri-cycle truck and drove it back off the road. He got out and gave the older man a command.

"Get their bags and go through them."

The older man walked over to the blue sedan and started removing the bags.

"It is so nice to meet English speaking tourists," said the young man. "It's good for keeping my language skills sharp. Feel free to correct me if I make a bad mistake."

"What are you going to do with us?" asked Yvonne.

"You won't be hurt," said the thief. "We just want your money and other things of value like the handgun and we'll be on our way."

The older man started going through Jim's carry-on and found the pictures.

"Now then, would you all be so kind as to take off any jewelry, watches, rings and money and place them in the bag," said the young man.

The older man tossed the pictures aside and one picture caught his eye. He picked it up and looked at it closely. It was a picture of Jim and a young Vietnamese boy taken twenty-five years earlier. The old man got up and called his young accomplice.

"Quang, come see this," yelled the older thief.

"Just a second," said the younger man. "Thank you all so much."

"Quang, please look at this."

The older man was almost hysterical. Jim was watching with keen interest. The younger man came over and took the picture. He stared at it the longest time. He turned to the three captives.

"Who is this man in the picture?" the young man screamed.

Jim looked at Yvonne in wonderment and turned back to the young thief.

"I guess that's me," he said meekly.

The young man stared at the picture again and then stared at Jim again with a look of concern.

"It can't be… Jim?"

At the sound of his name Jim was both shocked and confused. He couldn't understand what was happening. His voice broke, but he was not sure why.

"Yes, Jim," he answers.

"Jim!" the young man screamed, as a broad smile enveloped his face. "Jim, its Quang!"

Quang's arms went out in a welcome gesture, and he dropped the M-16. Jim's look of shock was beyond description.

*   *

A hot and humid tarmac at DaNang International Airport awaited the Air Vietnam flight from Bangkok. As the wheeled stairway was pushed into place and the door opened, the first passenger off the plane was the gangster with the shiny brass buckled shoes, dressed very smartly in a light blue suit, sunglasses, and tie. He walked to the terminal building where a police lieutenant assisted his passage through customs. The lieutenant gave the man an envelope with Vietnamese money, some papers and travel permits. The lieutenant bowed and walked away leaving the gangster to find his own bag at baggage claim.

The gangster didn't like coming to Vietnam, but this was a chance to solidify his place in Kai-Ling's Bangkok organization. He hated Chi Woo and relished the thought of getting one up on him. The papers he carried gave him authority over the Chinese thug. Chi Woo would have to take orders from him from now on, and he smiled every time he thought about it.

The gangster picked up his bag and walked to the taxi stand, getting the first one for the drive to the Green Plaza Hotel. Chi Woo would meet him there, and he looked forward to it.

The taxi made its way slowly through the busy afternoon traffic and pulled into the hotel driveway at 2:00 p.m. The man got out and paid the driver with a generous tip since it wasn't his money. The bell captain took his bag, and they walked inside the lobby. A Vietnamese man by the desk recognized the gangster and approached him.

"Where is Chi Woo?" asked the gangster. "He was supposed to be here."

"He sends his apologies, but he has driven to the village of Thuong Duc to retrieve the girl," said the Vietnamese man.

"Damn him!" said the gangster.

"He told me to tell you there was no reason to venture out to the village as he would have the girl back here by this evening," continued the Vietnamese man.

"No, that's not the way it's going to go down," said the gangster. "I need a car right away."

"I have a car here, but Mr. Woo will be extremely upset," said the man.

The gangster handed the Vietnamese man papers showing orders from Kai-Ling and his Vietnamese counterpart relieving Chi Woo of operational control.

"Very well," said the Vietnamese man. "You can leave immediately."

* *

Quang could not believe his eyes. He ran over to Jim and embraced him hard. Jim was in a state of confusion. What was this crazy man doing?

"Jim, Jim, my old friend, it's me, Quang!" exclaimed Quang.

He showed Jim the picture and pointed to himself as a boy.

"It's me, my old friend," said Quang. "You look older, but now I see it's you."

"Quang? What the hell? Quang…"

Jim couldn't believe his eyes at first or how much Quang has changed, but he finally realized that it really was Quang; Quang, the boy he had befriended all those years ago.

Then, with the ridiculousness of the situation bearing down on him, he yelled, "Quang, for Christ's sake, untie us!"

"No problem, Jim," Quang said and started fumbling with the ropes on Jim's wrists. He turned to the older thief and spoke in Vietnamese. "Uncle, put down the rifle and help me untie them."

Jim was the first to get untied, and he took Quang by the shoulders and shook him good-naturedly.

"Quang, I can't believe it's really you," said Jim, looking at him long and hard.

Yvonne stood and looked at the two old friends. She walked over and took the picture from Quang. Looking at it, she said, "Do you mean to tell me that this little boy in the picture is our bandit?"

"Yes, it's him. I can't believe it myself," said Jim. "What are you doing here? Where did you get these M-16's?"

Quang lowered his eyes, and then looked back up at Jim, his shoulders straightening. "I'm a business man and this is my business. I picked these rifles up off the battlefield years ago. I've got a cache near here with more M-16s and lots of bullets hidden and a small amount there on the mountain." Quang pointed up the side of the adjacent tall hill.

"Some of the rifles I have bought along with other Marine battle equipment. Canteens, belts, clothes, flak jackets. You name it," said Quang.

"So you're a thief? Didn't I teach you any better than that?" demanded Jim.

"Yes, a thief, but out of necessity, and a damn good one, too," said Quang. "I share my profits with the authorities, police and army. It's a good business for a non-communist. Haven't had to kill anyone and never got thrown in a cell. Now tell me, what are you doing here?"

"Well, I was returning to Thuong Duc to see the old place. I left in such a hurry, being wounded and all," said Jim.

"Wounded. I thought as much," said Quang. "Yes, that's why I became a thief. When you never returned, I had to steal food. The old women who lived with me died a short time later. I've been a thief ever since. Is she your wife?"  Quang nodded toward Yvonne.

Jim had completely forgotten to introduce Yvonne and Thanh. They both were untied and standing; Thanh still unsure of what was going on.

"No, she's a friend. A very good friend. This is Yvonne," said Jim. "Miss Chin, this is Quang."

Quang looked more closely at Yvonne after hearing her name and took her hand to shake it.

"Quang, nice to meet you, I think," said Yvonne.

"Miss Chin? Not Dr. Chin's daughter?" asked Quang.

Yvonne was a startled at the mention of her father's name, not sure she wanted a thief to know about him.

"Well..., yes," Yvonne hesitated. "Obviously you know of him."

"Oh, yes. Everyone knows of Dr. Chin in Thuong Duc, and of your grandmother, Mrs. Diem. And I know you, too," said Quang. "I remember you years ago before you left. You didn't look Vietnamese. You still don't."

"Yes, only part Vietnamese," returned Yvonne. "Would you know where my father is now?"

"Oh, yes. Some people know, but only the most trusted villagers. The police and soldiers at the camp don't even know. Come. I will take you there. Your family will be glad to see you."

Thanh walked over to the group rubbing his wrists that were sore from the ropes.

"Oh, Quang, this is Thanh, our driver," said Yvonne.

"Glad to meet you, Thanh. Sorry about this mix up," said Quang.

Thanh walked over to Quang and stood face to face, pointing at the old blue sedan.

"Take a very good look at me and my Peugeot," said Thanh. "Next time you see me, I expect that you will let me pass without incident."

"Of course," grinned Quang. "Any friend of Jim's is a friend of mine."

"Good!" said Thanh. "Okay then, I'm glad to meet you, too," and shook Quang's hand.

After they had a good handshake, the men started moving the fallen log back into its upright position. Quang had the older thief stash the M-16s in their cache on the side of the hill.

"I feel like an accomplice for your next robbery," said Jim.

"We only rob tourists and never hurt them. Besides, a lot of them say the robbery is the highlight of their visit to Vietnam," returned Quang. "Now you can follow me to the village."

Quang got into the three-wheeled truck and the older man got in the bed while Thanh started the Peugeot. When Jim and Yvonne put their bags back in the trunk, the two vehicles pulled out on to the main road. After half an hour of traveling up and down rises and passing streams and rice paddies, the group made its way into the Thuong Duc Valley where Jim started to recognize the countryside.

Nothing had really changed in twenty-five years with the exception of electric power poles alongside the road. These poles stuck out like a sore thumb, and Jim thought they were nothing more than an eyesore. They pushed on up the valley past the Old Catholic church, and soon the Song Vu Gia River appeared on their left and the old plateau, where the Special Forces camp was, rose above the village.

Jim got a faraway look and Yvonne noticed a little hint of redness around his eyes.

She took his hand as the old blue Peugeot pulled into the village.

"James, are you going to be okay?" she asked.

"This is unbelievable," said Jim. "It all looks the same. It just seems like it was yesterday."

The three-wheeled truck motored across a small bridge and entered the main part of the village as the Peugeot followed. Jim looked to the left as they made their way across the bridge.

"There's the old swimming hole."

Yvonne smiled as they passed sampans in the river, stilted houses, markets, and lots of children.

"Boy, the kids haven't changed either," said Jim.

Thanh drove past a boy riding a water buffalo and finally Quang, in the three-wheeled truck, stopped in front of a small concrete house with a thatched roof. As Jim and Yvonne got out they immediately drew a crowd of children. Quang hopped out of the truck and strode up to the front door. He knocked and Mrs. Diem answered the door.

"Yes, Quang, what do you want?" asked the old woman.

“Mrs. Diem, I have visitors,” said Quang, as he waved his arm toward Yvonne and Jim.

“Granddaughter!” the old woman cried.

“Grandmother,” smiled Yvonne.

Yvonne and her grandmother hugged and kissed as Jim was laughing with the kids. More adults recognized Yvonne and one of the older village men sent a teenage boy after more of the elders. Soon four older men showed up and drove the kids away. Yvonne and her grandmother entered the house along with the village elders and Quang pulled Jim inside with him.

“Thanh, wait out here with the car,” said Jim.

Thanh nodded and sat back in the driver’s seat, settling back to take a nap.

“Grandmother, it is good to see you,” said Yvonne in Vietnamese.

“And you, as well,” her grandmother replied.

Yvonne turned to the elders. “I have some bad news,” she said. “Where is father?”

“He’s across the river on the mountain. He’s not due back until tomorrow,” said the oldest man.

“An, the messenger was killed in DaNang,” Yvonne told them solemnly.

The old men looked at each other gravely.

"He was a trusted man. This is not good," said the old man.

"Father's life is in danger, and it is perilous for him to stay here any longer. We must leave as soon as possible," said Yvonne.

"Quang," said grandmother Diem. "Go as fast as you can and summon my son-in-law."

"Yes, maam," said Quang. "I need someone to take me across the river."

"Liem is always on his boat," said the elder. "Tell him what's going on and he will take you across and wait for you to return with Dr. Chin."

Quang nodded and smiled at Yvonne, then looked at Jim.

"I'll be back," he said and dashed out.

Jim had a look of confusion, and Yvonne realized that all the talk was in Vietnamese.

"He's going after my father. It may be a few hours," said Yvonne.

"Good. You need to relax and get some rest," said Jim.

The village elders interrupted and turned to go, promising to be nearby and to be of help when Dr. Chin returned. Yvonne was left inside with Jim and her grandmother. She turned back to Jim.

"How could I possibly relax?" Yvonne asked after the men had gone.

"Listen, old Chi Woo is probably in a hospital somewhere getting that slug you put in him taken out. He won't be here for a while, and besides, with the police here and the village behind you, he would be a fool to try anything," said Jim.

"Perhaps you're right," said Yvonne.

"Of course I'm right. When your father gets here we'll go to police headquarters and call Captain Minh," said Jim. "He'll see that you get out okay. Besides, he will do anything for you. He likes you."

"Captain Minh likes all women," said Yvonne. "You forget that we have the small problem of a shooting in the middle of DaNang to be concerned with. I think if we can get out of the country without the police knowing it would be better."

"At any rate, why don't you stay here and try to get some rest. I still have some business of my own to finish," said Jim. "I'll have Thanh drive me up to the police compound, and I can see what the old camp looks like now."

"Sure, of course, go ahead," said Yvonne.

Jim smiled at her and touched her hand, but she resisted, aware of her grandmother watching, and Jim realized her uneasiness.

"Grandmother, I forgot to introduce you to my friend James," said Yvonne in Vietnamese.

The grandmother smiled and said hello to Jim in Vietnamese.

"James, this is my grandmother, Mrs. Diem."

Jim was unsure of what to do and made a little bow as he took grandmother's hand.

"Is it okay to shake hands?" he asked Yvonne.

"She grew up with the French, so I think if you kissed her hand that would show your respect."

"Nice to meet you, Mrs. Diem," said Jim, as he kissed her hand lightly.

"James, I couldn't possibly relax," said Yvonne. "Are you sure you don't want me to come with you? You probably should have someone with you."

Jim hesitated a beat and all the old feelings of war and all it entailed started to well up inside him.

“Well, if you’re sure you don’t mind, maybe it would be nice to have a hand to hold,” said Jim.

Yvonne explained to her grandmother what they were going to do and why. Jim bowed goodbye, and they departed the small concrete house.

Thanh had been trying to sleep, but with little success and was startled at the knock on the window.

“Should I make plans for staying the night?” asked Thanh.

“I don’t think so,” said Jim.

“I hope to leave for DaNang as soon as my father returns in a few hours,” added Yvonne.

“Right now I need you to drive me up to the police compound on the hill,” said Jim.

“You going to report that bandit?” asked Thanh.

“No, no. I have something else in mind,” said Jim.

Jim and Yvonne took their seats in the back of the Peugeot, and Thanh turned the car around. They wound along the narrow village road and took the fork up the hill to the old Special Forces camp. The river opened before them as they climbed and Jim remembered how beautiful the view was. Many small trees and bushes had taken root in the red rocky soil and the center road was rutted from many torrential rains. They reached the top of the horseshoe-shaped plateau and Thanh came to a stop next to the police compound gate.

"Stay to the left. Don't go to the gate," said Jim. "Pull up right here."

Thanh turned to the left and stopped the Peugeot. Jim got out first and took his time looking around.

"What are we doing here?" asked Thanh as he turned back to Yvonne.

"Just wait and you will see. Come, let's get out with him."

Thanh and Yvonne got out and watched as Jim walked a few feet to the west and entered a flat grassy area with a graveyard beyond. He turned to Yvonne.

"This is the old helicopter landing zone," said Jim. "And look, they made a graveyard up here. How apropos!"

He walked back toward the car continuing his remembrances.

"There would have been a ditch right about here and many small sand bagged bunkers. The Green Berets were on the right side where the police compound is now, and we Marines were on the left side over there, commanding a view of the river all the way to the South China Sea."

"I think I remember that day," Yvonne said slowly, "although there were so many days with explosions and small arms fire."

Jim knelt down at the edge of the old landing zone and picked up some of the loose dirt. Thanh, confused, asked Yvonne in Vietnamese what was going on. She turned to him and whispered, "James was in the war here."

Thanh nodded understandingly.

"This is where it happened," Jim said, starting to choke up. "As far as I can tell, this is where I was wounded, right here on this spot. I…"

His eyes welled up, and he couldn't hold the emotion any longer. He sobbed heavily. Yvonne went over to him and knelt beside him, putting her hand on his shoulder.

"For three days we stayed underground," she said. "It was not long after that when my father was smuggled in and we left this village."

Jim was trying to compose himself. He wiped his face on the back of his sleeve. He was glad Yvonne had come with him; it was something that needed to be done with compassion and support.

"I thought I would be okay coming back here," said Jim. "I didn't know I would feel this bad. We were all so young. So many young men ... so many on both sides. They never had a chance at life like I had." His voice was just a whisper.

Across the way in the police compound Lieutenant Nguyen, the police commander, had come outside and noticed the blue Peugeot parked beyond the gate. He walked over to the sentry and stood next to him watching the American kneeling in the grass.

"Who are they? What are they doing here?" the lieutenant asked.

"I don't know, sir. They drove up a minute ago," said the sentry.

The lieutenant straightened and strode toward Jim and Yvonne.

"I just can't understand how anyone can send off a bunch of nineteen-year-olds to fight a war," said Jim. "I mean all you have to do is go to any high school and see how young they look....The only thing it did was make a bunch of weapons manufacturers rich and the rest of us scared for life."

"Who are you and want do you want?" yelled Lieutenant Nguyen in Vietnamese.

Jim and Yvonne were surprised at the sound of the lieutenant's voice, and they looked up to see who was there.

"Do you have business here?" the lieutenant continued in a stern voice.

Yvonne stood first while Jim wiped his eyes, again embarrassed at being in front of the police commander.

"Lieutenant," Yvonne addressed the commander in Vietnamese. "This is Dr. Braden, an American doctor who fought in the war twenty-five years ago."

The lieutenant watched Jim as he got to his feet. His demeanor was cold, and he continued to be tough.

"What is he doing here?" asked the lieutenant again.

"What is he saying?" interrupted Jim.

"No need," said the lieutenant as he raised his arm to stop Yvonne from answering. "I speak English."

"Good. I'm Jim Braden, and I was stationed here myself, twenty-five years ago," said Jim, as he offered his hand in an attempt to break the ice.

The lieutenant made no move to shake hands. Jim was taken back and embarrassed by his sobbing earlier, but he kept on smiling.

“I have a letter from Captain Minh,” said Jim. “This should explain everything.”

Jim dug the letter out of his shirt pocket and handed it to the lieutenant who began to read it.

“Where are your passports and travel permits?” demanded the lieutenant, to both Jim and Yvonne.

“They’re in the car,” said Yvonne, in a sharp tone of her own.

“And you, driver, get your license and tourist permit,” added Lieutenant Nguyen to Thanh.

Jim and Yvonne retreated to the back seat of the Peugeot while Thanh turned so the lieutenant couldn’t see and made a sarcastic face before reaching in the passenger side door to retrieve his papers from the glove box. Jim returned with both his and Yvonne’s papers.

“Here you go,” said Jim, as he handed the passports and papers over to the lieutenant.

The lieutenant looked over the passports and permits and turned toward Yvonne.

“Yvonne Chin?”

“Yes,” said Yvonne.

"Dr. Chin's daughter?" asked the lieutenant.

Yvonne paused wondering how this non-villager policeman knew of her father. "Well, yes, my father's last name is Chin," said Yvonne with a slight mocking tone.

The lieutenant was irritated by this remark, but he held his temper. He turned back to Jim.

"Dr. Braden, this is a provincial police compound. Captain Minh has no authority out here. Only I do. I will keep your permits and passports for the time being. In the meantime go away from here and stay in the village," said the lieutenant. "You, driver, give me your papers."

Thanh strolled over to the lieutenant in no particular hurry and handed him his papers.

"Driver, see that you don't leave this village until I say so," said Lieutenant Nguyen.

The lieutenant turned to the guard and spoke in Vietnamese.

"Get three officers and station them at the bridge head. See that no cars or trucks leave the village without my order."

The lieutenant walked back to the police compound without looking back.

"What the hell is his problem?" asked Jim.

"I'm not sure, but he isn't helping matters. We need those passports to get out of here," said Yvonne.

"He's an asshole," said Thanh.

"Come on, let's go," said Jim. "Not quite what I expected in the way of returning, but I found my spot. I can look around with no one shooting, and I had my cry."

They all returned to the Peugeot and drove back to Mrs. Diem's house. Lieutenant Nguyen watched intently as they left the hill.

Back in the village, Mrs. Diem and the rest of the villagers close to her had started an impromptu celebration for Yvonne. Children were doing a dance while women were setting up cooking places next to the grandmother's house. Before long everyone was having a joyous time and the rude Lieutenant Nguyen was forgotten for the time being. Jim had produced his notebook and started drawing cartoons for the kids, becoming a regular hit.

Yvonne was watching him and smiling as her grandmother snuggled up beside her. She kissed Yvonne's cheek.

"I hope father gets here soon," Yvonne said, continuing to look at Jim.

Grandmother Diem noticed her look and remembered her own looks many years ago in regards to another young man.

"You care for this man, don't you?" she asked.

"Oh, Grandmother," said Yvonne, seeing the glint in her eye. "Stop it, he's just a friend."

"Okay, if you say so," she said. "The children like him, and he likes them."

"He's a children's doctor. He delivers babies so he's supposed to like children," said Yvonne.

"That's not what I mean," returned the grandmother.

They looked at each other and smiled.

*     *

# Chapter 10

Quang jumped into the knee-deep water as Liem guided the open sampan into shore on the south side of the Song Vu Gia River.

"You know the place on the mountain, right?" asked Liem.

"I know, the old NVA cave where they hid mortars and food," answered Quang. "The one on the left path."

"Yes, that's the one. Be quick," said Liem.

Quang took a machete knife he had taken from the three-wheeled truck and set off on the path to the base of the mountain. Years before no one ever came to this side of the river. During the war not even the Americans ventured beyond this point with the exception of the Green Berets and their South Vietnamese Rangers.

This was NVA territory. The badlands where the beast of war would dwell in silence, invisible, watching the American Marines on the other side of the river. They waited for the chance to lay down mortar and recoilless rifle fire and then blended back into the jungle. So it went; the NVA invisible day or night and the Marines, conversely, visible targets at all times.

Quang continued climbing the left path for an hour when he heard a sound ahead and froze in his tracks.

"Men of Thuong Duc, its Quang. I'm alone," called the young man.

In a moment a head and body cautiously peered around a tree ahead and surveyed the path.

"Quang, come on," the voice called back.

The young man walked softly forward and came abreast of the guard with an AK-47 rifle.

"Go on up to the cave," said the guard. "I'll be staying here to make sure you weren't followed."

Quang continued another hundred meters and came to a broad level area in front of a large cave mouth. Dr. Chin, sitting on a rock eating some fruit, looked up at him.

"I recognize you, but I forget your name," said Dr. Chin.

Quang noticed another village man with a rifle walk out of the cave.

"It's Quang, the thief," said the man.

"Oh yes," said Dr. Chin. "Now I remember; the Robin Hood boy."

"Yes," said Quang. "You called me that before, a long time ago," said Quang.

"That's because you rob the rich and give to the poor," said Dr. Chin. "Mostly you are a good one, and I've heard you help the village poor."

"Why are you here, Quang?" asked the village man.

"Dr. Chin's daughter is here. She says you are in great danger and wants to take you away from here," answered Quang.

"Yvonne? So soon? I didn't expect her for another week," said the doctor.

"She has a car and driver and wants you to come quickly," said Quang.

The doctor looked concerned.

"You'd better be telling the truth, Quang!" said the villager with the rifle.

"I am. I'm trustworthy. I'm part of this village, too."

"Okay, let me get my things," said Dr. Chin. "We'll take the long path back to make sure he wasn't followed or tricked into this. Go get the other guard and return. I'll get my things packed."

*     *

Thanh was going from cooking pot to cooking pot sampling all the good food and enjoying his free time. The whole scene was festive and Jim and Yvonne were having a good time as well in spite of their tension.

The sounds of a car horn grew louder and louder, and soon Jim saw a police jeep-like truck honking at villagers to make way as it drove up the road and stopped at the Diem house. Yvonne looked concerned and the joyous mood of the party faded quickly. A policeman got out and approached Yvonne speaking in Vietnamese.

"You, come with me," barked the policeman to Yvonne. "Get up now!"

Jim, looking concerned, stood up beside Yvonne.

"American, too, and grandmother," demanded the policeman. "Let's go."

"What's going on here?" said Yvonne.

"Lieutenant Nguyen wants to see all of you, said the policeman. "Now!"

"What did he say?" asked Jim.

Yvonne conveyed the order as the villagers looked on wondering what was happening. Jim, Yvonne, and Grandmother Diem got into the Peugeot, and Thanh, still stuffing the last bits of food in his mouth, got in the driver's seat. The policeman waved them around and then followed them to the compound.

"I don't like this," said Yvonne.

"Maybe we should make a break for it," said Jim.

"No, maybe if father was with us, but now we have to wait and see what this arrogant jerk wants," said Yvonne. "Maybe it's nothing."

They continued up the hill and through the gate, parking next to a familiar black sedan with a bullet hole in the driver's side rear window. Yvonne looked at Jim, and they both looked at the car.

"Chi Woo," said Jim.

"James, let me do the talking," pleaded Yvonne with her sternest glare. "I mean it; promise me."

"Okay, I promise," said Jim.

Jim, Yvonne, and Grandmother Diem got out and walked inside the headquarters office with the policeman following. As they entered the office the first thing they saw was Mr. Summerpot sitting at the side of the compound commander's desk in deep conversation with the lieutenant.

"Mr. Summerpot, thank God it's you," said Jim.

"Yes, thanks indeed," said Summerpot, his gaze fixed beyond Jim. "My boy, and Yvonne, how nice to see you're both well."

Summerpot stood and walked past Jim and Yvonne, barely acknowledging them, moving toward the old woman.

"I see you've brought someone with you," continued Summerpot. "Madam, how are you?"

Summerpot took the old woman's hand and grasped it firmly, looked her right in the eye and patted her shoulder. Grandmother Diem was expressionless and made no movement. Summerpot continued to look at her in a reassuring way. Without looking back at her, Summerpot spoke to Yvonne.

"Just to make things absolutely clear," continued the fat man, "Tell me my dear, who is this old woman to you?"

Yvonne hesitated, wondering why he was interested in her grandmother. When no response came, Summerpot turned around to face her.

"Yvonne, did you hear me?" said Summerpot.

"Yes, of course. This is my grandmother, Mrs. Diem," said Yvonne.

"You don't say," replied Summerpot. "So this is your grandmother."

The fat man turned back around to Mrs. Diem and she stared deeply into his eyes, but made no move.

"Charming woman," said Summerpot.

Summerpot turned back around to face everyone in the room with the grandmother at his back.

"Well, I suppose you are both wondering how I got here," said the fat man.

"Yes, how did you get here?" asked Jim.

Before he could answer, a door in the back of the office opened with a *creak* that caught everyone's attention.

"He came with me," said a voice in the shadow of the doorway.

A man turned around in the darkness of the back bathroom, and Chi Woo limped out of the shadows in the back of the office. His left leg and foot below the knee were wrapped in a large bandage; his arm was bandaged, too. At the same time, Chi Woo's Vietnamese henchmen came in the front office door and blocked it.

"Miss Chin, how nice. Just the person I was looking for," said the Chinese gangster. "And your father? Is he near?"

Jim and Yvonne were shocked, and Mrs. Diem confused. They turned to look at Summerpot and he shrugged with a smirk on his face as if to say I'm sorry, I like you both, but this is business.

"Mr. Summerpot, this man is a gangster," said Jim.

"I know my boy, so I suggest you do whatever he says."

Jim turned to the lieutenant.

"I demand that you call Captain Minh in DaNang," said Jim.

The lieutenant had a blank look on his face and sat back in his chair making no move toward the phone on his desk. Chi Woo walked over to Jim and smiled. Without warning he slapped Jim across the face with the back of his good hand. Jim staggered back from the blow, and then every memory of any bully he had ever known came to him in a split second, and he lunged at Chi Woo knocking him back on the lieutenant's desk. One of the henchmen moved forward and clubbed Jim on the head, sending him to the floor.

Chi Woo got back up and straightened himself out, smoothing his suit coat. He took a step toward Jim and then violently kicked him in the ribs. Jim curled over on the floor, ringed with pain.

"Stop it!" screamed Yvonne. "Lieutenant, do your duty and stop this."

Chi Woo turned to Yvonne and smiled and then turned back to the lieutenant and laughed.

"It will do you no good to yell at the lieutenant or call Captain Minh. You see, the good lieutenant and I have an agreement and Captain Minh is not here," said Chi Woo. "And Mr. Summerpot enjoys money and the many benefits of helping my organization from time to time."

Summerpot was growing restless, and he had not enjoyed seeing what had just transpired.

"Well, I see my job is done. I'll be returning to DaNang now," said Summerpot. "Mr. Woo, if you don't mind I think I'll commandeer Miss Chin's car and driver. I trust you will provide for them."

“You pig!” exclaimed Yvonne.

Summerpot was noticeably upset by this remark. Turning away from Yvonne and stepping toward Mrs. Diem, he took her hand once more and spoke softly in Vietnamese.

“Don’t worry all will be well.”

As Summerpot left the office, Chi Woo walked over to Yvonne.

“Now then, Miss Chin. About your father.”

* *

Summerpot moved outside and walked over to the old blue Peugeot where Thanh was trying to stay calm. Some police officers were talking nearby.

“Why did I have to take this job? Police, gangsters, thieves, I don’t know. I should retire,” said Thanh to himself.

“My good man,” said Summerpot as he tapped on the driver’s door. “Time to get going; I need you to take me back to DaNang.”

Thanh looked at the fat man like he was crazy and shrugged.

“I got a client all ready. Miss Chin and Jim,” said Thanh.

"They no longer need your services. I do," said Summerpot.

"No, I can't leave them here, and besides, my license and permit are with the lieutenant," said Thanh.

Summerpot had no time to argue so he pulled out a wad of bills and handed them to Thanh.

"If that isn't incentive enough, maybe this will make you see it my way," said Summerpot as he pulled back his coat lapel and gave Thanh a look at a small caliber handgun neatly tucked inside. "Don't make me use this."

"What about them?" asked Thanh, as he pointed to the policemen at the gate.

"They're on my side," said Summerpot.

The fat man yelled at the policemen to open the gate. By now they all knew that Chi Woo and Summerpot had the freedom to come and go, and they opened the gate. He got in the back and the old blue sedan drove down the hill.

"You need to get me to a phone fast," said Summerpot, as he leaned forward in the back seat.

Thanh turned to nod in agreement and then jerked the car to the right forcefully and skidded to a halt throwing Summerpot into the back of the front seat.

"What the hell are you doing," yelled Summerpot as he straightened up.

"It's not me," cried Thanh. "It's that crazy thief, Quang."

"Thief," said Summerpot.

Summerpot looked outside and sure enough Quang's three-wheeled truck was stopped almost sideways in the road after screeching to a halt and almost throwing Dr. Chin out the back. It was less than a foot from the Peugeot's front bumper. Thanh yelled out the window at Quang.

"Why do you drive so fast? You could have smashed my car."

Quang looked and, not seeing Jim or Yvonne, yelled, "Who's that guy and where's Jim?"

Dr. Chin got out of the back and walked forward brushing himself off. Summerpot recognized the doctor and quickly got out of the Peugeot.

"Dr. Chin, its Summerpot," said the fat man.

"My goodness, it is," said Dr. Chin in amazement. "I haven't seen you in over twenty years. How did you know my name?"

“There’s no time for that now,” said Summerpot. “Yvonne’s in trouble at the police compound, and you are in danger.”

“What about Jim?” demanded a concerned Quang.

Summerpot looked at Quang in a bit of confusion wondering how he knew about Dr. Braden, but answered anyway.

“He is in trouble, too.”

“Come on, let’s go help him. I know the lieutenant. He will listen to me,” said Quang.

“You don’t understand my boy. These men are heavily armed murderers and the lieutenant is with them,” said Summerpot. “Dr. Chin, you trusted me twenty years ago to smuggle you in and out of this country, and I didn’t even know your name then. You must trust me now.”

“I must protect my daughter, Mr. Summerpot,” said Dr. Chin as he turned to go.

The fat man grabbed his arm and stopped him.

“If you go in there, fine, but I need time first. I need to get to the nearest phone and call my friend Captain Minh. We need weapons and men to use them.”

“I have weapons,” said Quang.

Summerpot looked at him in disbelief.

"I do," said Quang. "M-16s."

"What? …Where?" asked a baffled Summerpot.

"About twenty minutes down the road, just before the river checkpoint. There's a phone there too," said Quang.

"Okay, you're coming with me… Dr. Chin wait one hour and then go to the police compound," said Summerpot.

"What if they hurt her before?" asked Dr. Chin.

"They won't harm her. They want you and they know you would tell them nothing if she were hurt. Mrs. Diem is there, too, and this Jim that the boy spoke of has become a delight for me, so I want to save them all."

"Okay, one hour, no more," said Dr. Chin.

Summerpot and Quang got in the Peugeot and Dr. Chin backed up the three-wheeled truck letting Thanh drive the old sedan out of the village.

*    *

# Chapter 11

Chi Woo's men had tied Jim, bloody and aching, to a chair in the middle of the lieutenant's office. Yvonne and her grandmother were huddled together along the back wall. Chi Woo lifted Jim's head and started to slap him again, but Yvonne objected.

"Stop it! Leave him alone," she cried.

The lieutenant looked on in enjoyment as Chi Woo took a step toward Yvonne.

"Miss Chin, I'm enjoying this immensely, but I fear you have little compassion for such fun," said Chi Woo. "Would you rather I try it on the old woman?"

"You scum bag," said Jim groggily.

Chi Woo slapped him again. Yvonne got up and hit Chi Woo, and he raised his arm to strike her.

"Go ahead, hit me," screamed Yvonne. "My father will never give you what you want if he sees me hurt."

Chi Woo hesitated and thought that she may be right. He remembered the warning Summerpot gave him about hurting her at all, for if he did Dr. Chin would take his research with him to the grave.

"You make a good point," smiled Chi Woo. "But don't try my patience too much."

*  *

The old blue Peugeot was moving as fast as Thanh could make it go over the rough red road, horn blaring to warn the few pedestrians and the even fewer motor scooters that happened to be in its way.

Quang related the story of how Jim and he became friends and how he came to rob them earlier in the day. This made Summerpot chuckle for a moment, but the seriousness of their predicament squelched the humor swiftly. Quang and Summerpot had no plan other than to let Quang get his weapons out of the cache and in firing condition while Summerpot made the phone call to Captain Minh.

"Here it is," called Quang, from the back seat as they reached the area where Quang's first cache was located.

"I know, I know," said Thanh. "You robbed me here this morning, remember. You think I have forgotten?"

"Mr. Summerpot, I have two M-16s and ammo here on this hill and more at another hiding place about two miles past the checkpoint."

The blue sedan pulled to the side of the road and Quang jumped out.

"You get those two rifles ready, and I'll send Thanh right back with the car," said Summerpot. "I've got to make that phone call first."

"Okay, I'll be ready in ten minutes," said Quang.

As the car sped off he waved goodbye before starting up the hill at a brisk pace.

A few minutes later Summerpot and Thanh arrived at the police check point near the river village and started across the bridge. Another car, a Datsun B-210 that had been stopped at the checkpoint, was just heading toward them, driving fast. The narrowness of the bridge made it necessary for Thanh to pull far to the right and slow down as the other car sped past.

"What is his problem?" said Thanh. "I should never have gotten out of bed this morning."

"Me either," said Summerpot.

The blue Peugeot pulled up just before the checkpoint, and Summerpot got out to approach the guards as Thanh backed the car around and hurried back across the bridge. The guards, with their AK-47s shouldered, wondered what was going on. They were the same two guards from earlier in the day. The first guard recognized the car and Mr. Summerpot, but not the two of them together.

"I need your phone, young man, it's an emergency," said Summerpot.

The guard was not impressed.

"The phone is for official business," said the young guard.

"This is official business," said Summerpot, pulling out his handgun and putting it to the neck of the smaller guard. "Take me to the phone and you will be glad you did."

The young man, with his weapon on his shoulder and his comrade busy with another vehicle, walked Summerpot over to the small outpost office.

"Pick up the phone and dial DaNang police headquarters and ask for Captain Minh," instructed Summerpot.

"Captain Minh?" said the surprised guard.

"Yes, I told you it was official business. Now hurry."

The guard dialed and waited for Captain Minh to come on the line.

"Captain Minh here," said the voice on the phone.

The young guard handed it to Summerpot.

"Tran, its Summerpot. Listen; there's been a change in plans. I know why Chi Woo wants the girl now, and your Lieutenant Nguyen has taken a bribe from him in exchange for his help."

"What, the. . .? That stupid imbecile! What can we do?" asked Captain Minh.

"I need you out here with some men to take out Chi Woo. I will be in your debt and do whatever I can for you if you can help me. For the girl's sake. You know why!" said Summerpot.

"I can't use policemen. It would be too unexplainable to my superiors," said Tran Minh.

"If it will help, I have a source of American M-16 rifles and ammunition," said Summerpot.

"What?"

"Yes, you heard correctly," continued the fat man.

"Okay, I have an idea," said Captain Minh. "I should be there in an hour if all goes well."

"Good, but hurry," said Summerpot.

The fat man was about to hang up when he realized he still had a gun held on the young police guard.

"One more thing, Tran. Talk to your guard and tell him I'm working with you."

* *

Kai-Ling's handpicked gangster drove the Datsun B-210 as fast as he could, heading for Thuong Duc. He was fuming at the thought of Chi Woo beating him to the girl and her father. He watched and tried to keep the Chinese thug out of his mind as rice paddies whizzed past. Green pastures, with the reddish-brown cattle of Vietnam, grazing beside small streams, seemed so serene in a country that had been torn by wartime more often than peacetime.

The gangster's car rushed past the young thief's hillside cave, and Quang heard the car below from quite a distance away. He stopped his cleaning and peered through the jungle foliage to get a glimpse of it. So many cars this particular day and so much trouble.

He went back to his cleaning and soon had both M-16s in firing order. He filled two magazines for each and found two metal ammo boxes with more rounds.

Quang carried the ammo down the hill first and left it hidden in the bushes not far from the side of the road. He climbed back up the hill and strapped on both M-16s, one on each shoulder, and started back down with nothing to do now but wait for Thanh to return. He didn't have to wait long. Thanh turned in the side road, and they loaded the rifles in the trunk.

"Okay, let's get going," said Quang. I've got more down the road.

* *

Captain Minh hung up the phone and called to his aide. "Get me that old unmarked panel truck. The one we use to move prisoners at times."

"I know the one. I'll get a driver," said the aide.

"No, get it yourself. Park it out front and leave the keys in it," said the captain.

The aide followed orders, and Captain Minh went to his office to get his automatic handgun. He loaded it with a fresh magazine and took a spare out of the desk drawer, then walked out of the building.

The aide was just pulling the old Ford panel truck up to the curb and got out. “How much petrol does it have in it?” asked Captain Minh.

“Nearly full, sir,” said the aide.

“Good, I’ll be gone some time, maybe over night,” said Captain Minh.

“Yes, sir,” the aide replied as he turned away.

The captain got in the truck and started the motor. The aide turned back and stopped the captain.

“Sir, what should I say if someone is looking for you?”

The captain paused a second before replying.

“Tell them I went sightseeing for the rest of the afternoon.”

Captain Minh smiled and drove away. It did not take him long to get to the hotel district near the Han River and he quickly found one of the men he was looking for: a pedi-cab driver. He drove to the curb and stopped the pedi-cab driver who in turn recognized the captain.

“Where is sergeant Vien?” asked the captain.

"Last I saw he was headed up north to the vegetable market," said the ex-ranger.

"Has he talked with you and your comrades about working for me?" asked the captain.

"Yes, sir."

"Good! Take your cab and find the other ex-Rangers and return to the cab yard. I will meet you there after I find Sergeant Vien, now hurry," ordered Captain Minh.

"Yes, sir!" said the ex-ranger, as he smartly saluted the captain and peddled off.

Captain Minh was surprised by the salute, but enjoyed it. He was beginning to like these rangers more all the time.

* *

Chi Woo was losing his patience, and the pain in his leg was making him even more irritable. Jim was staring at him, still tied to the chair, and Yvonne and her grandmother huddled with one another in the back of the office. Lieutenant Nguyen was happy doing nothing except thinking of how he would spend the money Chi Woo had given him and hoping to do more business with the drug lords.

"Lieutenant," Chi Woo finally broke the silence. "I'm growing tired of this waiting. Take your men and go to the village. Tell everyone I am holding Dr. Chin's daughter and will kill her if he doesn't show up soon."

Lieutenant Nguyen was not happy at this order, but he had sold himself to this gangster so he got up and ordered his men to follow. Chi Woo turned to his henchmen when they left and ordered them to go with the lieutenant to make sure he followed orders. He was soon alone with Yvonne, Jim, and Mrs. Diem.

Another fifteen minutes passed and Chi Woo started to pace in a painful hobble. He stopped in front of Jim and stared at his bloody face.

"Dr. Braden, do you now wish you hadn't interfered with me back in Bangkok?"

Jim just glared at Chi Woo.

"You realize after Dr. Chin arrives that I will have no further use for you. I must tell you that I will make it as slow a death as possible. You should have never angered me," said Chi Woo.

The sound of a car pulling up outside made Chi Woo stare at the door, wondering if it was Dr. Chin.

“Perhaps the good doctor is here now,” he said.

Blam!

The front door burst open and in walked non-other than Larry Brewster. He had a handgun pointed at Chi Woo. The Chinese gangster was speechless as was Jim.

“Drop the gun, Woo,” said Larry.

Chi Woo dropped his gun, and it hit the floor without traveling far from his feet.

“Kick it over here,” said Larry.

Chi Woo kicked the gun toward Larry and locked eyes with him. Larry bent down to pick up the gun and kept his eyes on Chi Woo.

“Now, Miss Chin,” said Larry. “Untie Jim while I keep my eye on this son-of-a-bitch.”

Yvonne went to Jim and began untying him.

“What are you doing here?” demanded Chi Woo.

“Just come to see my old friend Jimbo,” said Larry. “Hey, Jimbo, you don’t look so good. Here this will help.”

Larry tossed Chi Woo’s gun to Jim who caught it with his free hand. Chi Woo took a split second to look back at the gun flying through the air and when he did, Larry seized the opportunity to hit him hard with a right cross, knocking him to the floor, out cold.

"Larry, I don't know how you got here, but I've never been so glad to see anyone," said Jim.

"Jimbo, I've never known anyone who can get into trouble like you. Come on, let's get out of here before he wakes up," said Larry.

Larry helped Yvonne untie Jim the rest of the way and got him on his feet. Yvonne went to get her grandmother who had been silent the whole time.

"Wait, James!" Yvonne cried. "My father."

Larry was heading to the front door and placed his hand on the knob.

"Larry, wait. We need to get her dad," said Jim.

"No problem," said Larry as he opened the door and a man walked in. "Dr. Chin, I presume."

"Larry how did you…" started Jim.

"Father," cried Yvonne.

"Yvonne, my dear," smiled Dr. Chin, rushing to her with outstretched arms.

"Hey, I just found him walking through the gate when I drove up," said Larry. "He was looking for you guys, and I convinced him to let me surprise you first."

"Mr. Brewster, how can I thank you?" asked Yvonne.

"Just get everyone in the car," said Larry. "We better be moving."

Jim herded Yvonne's grandmother out the door, and Yvonne and her father followed. Larry was left inside and pulled a silencer from his coat pocket and screwed it on the barrel of his gun. He walked back to Chi woo, pointed the gun at Chi Woo's head, and pulled the trigger. Larry looked down at the pool of blood on the floor.

"Stupid asshole," Larry said out loud. "No one fucks with me or my friends."

Larry Brewster replaced the silencer and the pistol in his coat pocket and left the office.

* *

Captain Minh, still in his police uniform, opened the back door to the old panel truck and got in. He sat on the right side bench and lit a cigar before addressing Cao.

"You drive, Sergeant Vien. The rest of you ride back here with me," said the captain.

As the ranger squad filed in the back of the truck with their Bermuda shorts and red *Life's a Bitch* tee shirts, the captain shook his head in disbelief, wondering if he was making a wise choice. The captain took a long drag on his cigar and sat back smiling at the four ex-Rangers. Cao started the motor and the old panel truck took off in a cloud of blue smoke.

*   *

Summerpot looked for Thanh and the old blue Peugeot, but they were still out of sight. He walked away from the gate barrier and took a seat in the vacant checkpoint office. Summerpot took his hat off and fanned his face offering some relief from the late afternoon sun. Soon the blue sedan rumbled across the bridge and pulled to a stop in front of the fat man.

"Where did the two police guards go?" asked Thanh through the open window.

"Captain Minh didn't want any more police around than necessary, so he told them to pack up early and come back to headquarters," said Summerpot. "They had their motor scooters behind the office here and are long gone."

"What do we do now?" asked Thanh.

"Take the young man to his other hiding place up the road and wait for Captain Minh. He shouldn't be long."

"Are you coming with us?" asked Quang.

"No, I'm the new crossing guard. I need to wait by the phone," said Summerpot. "Now get going and if no one shows up after a half hour come back and get me."

"Okay," said Quang and the Peugeot headed up the hill and out of sight.

Summerpot walked over to the little market to get something to eat and some Hanoi beer. He came back and lowered the red and white painted gate barrier, and returned to the guard office. The fat man sat back down, removing his gun and placing it on the desk not sure what might happen next.

* *

Larry came out of the office and went over to Chi Woo's car looking at the ignition.

"The keys are still in Chi Woo's car," said Larry. "Let's take his. It's bigger than the Datsun."

"Yvonne, you and your grandmother get in the back with Dr. Chin, and I'll ride in front with Larry," said Jim.

"Jimbo, you drive," said Larry. "I better ride shotgun."

Everyone piled into the car and Jim started the engine. He drove out of the police compound and saw the lieutenant and his men returning up the hill road.

"Punch it!" yelled Larry as he fired a shot from his revolver.

Jim hit the gas pedal and the big black car sped past the police and the two henchmen, scattering them like bowling pins as they jumped out of the way.

Lieutenant Nguyen got back up and ran into the compound. He saw the Datsun B-210 and ran inside the office. Chi Woo's henchmen followed. They found Chi Woo lying on the floor in a pool of dark red blood.

"We must catch them," said the first henchman. "Much is at stake."

The lieutenant hesitated, not sure of what to do. He had just lost the rest of his money.

"Lieutenant," said the henchman. "That Chinaman is very big and important man. His boss will pay us all well if we get that girl and her father."

The other policemen rushed in the door and were shocked by the dead body.

Lieutenant Nguyen turned to his men and gave an order.

"You, get me the truck and give me your AK-47." He pointed to a second officer. "Give me yours, too." He took the two rifles and motioned to the two henchmen.

"You two come with me. The rest of you clean up this mess."

The lieutenant and the two henchmen rushed outside where Lieutenant Nguyen gave the two thugs the AK-47s. The truck was pulled around and the lieutenant got in the driver's seat, shouldering his officer out of the way. The two thugs joined him inside the cab.

"Get rid of that body and do nothing else until I return," yelled Lieutenant Nguyen at his officer.

The truck rushed out of the police compound and down the hill into the village.

* *

# Chapter 12

Thanh was sitting in his Peugeot that was parked in the middle of the road. He was drinking a bottle of beer he had stashed in the glove box while Quang leaned against the front hood of the car. The few passers-by on the road looked at them in confusion, wondering what the two men were up to.

Not knowing what kind of vehicle Captain Minh would be driving, Quang and Thanh sat in the main road next to the cutoff that led to Quang's hiding place.

It was only a short while before the old Ford panel truck came into view. Quang spotted it first and turned back to Thanh.

"Get ready," said Quang. "This could be it."

Thanh nodded and set his beer down on the floorboard.

Cao saw Thanh's Peugeot from a distance and knew whose it was. He pulled up short of the blue sedan and jumped out. Thanh jumped out, too, and met him.

"Remind me never to do any favors for you again," said Thanh. "At any price."

"What has happened?" asked Cao. "The car looks good."

"I've been shot at, robbed…."

"No," interrupted Quang. "I never shot at you and it was a mistaken, attempted robbery."

Thanh gave Quang a dirty look and continued, "…tied-up, arrested, commandeered, and I'm not sure what else. And I haven't got the rest of my fee yet!"

The back door of the panel truck opened and Captain Minh jumped out. He hurried toward the men between the vehicles.

"Sergeant Vien, I recognize the driver from this morning, but don't know his name. Who is this young man?"

"Captain, this is Thanh, he owns the car and this is …?" said Cao, pointing at Quang.

"I'm Quang, a good friend of Dr. Braden, and we're wasting time."

"You have the weapons nearby?" asked the captain.

"Yes, follow us," said Quang.

"No, I'll ride with you two in the car. Sergeant Vien, you follow in the truck," ordered Captain Minh.

They all jumped back in the vehicles and turned off the side road toward Quang's hideout.

"Tell me Quang, how do you know Dr. Braden?" asked the captain, as he settled in to the more comfortable seat of the Peugeot.

"Jim and I met many years ago in Thuong Duc village. I was just a boy and orphaned. He helped feed me."

"And how did you get these weapons?"

Quang paused, knowing he might be incriminating himself.

"Are you going to arrest me?" he said.

"Probably not, but you know I can't let you keep them," said Captain Minh.

Quang, who didn't answer, was looking ahead and suddenly yelled at Thanh to make a right turn into a cow path. They continued a few hundred meters slightly upward to where the path ended in a grove of banana trees on a small rise above the rice paddies. Quang and the captain got out and the panel truck pulled up behind them.

"This way," said Quang. "It's just a short way."

Cao got out of the truck and followed Quang and the captain. The rest of the ex-Ranger squad got out of the back and stood by the truck. Thanh drank the rest of his beer that he had held between his thighs while driving.

Quang made his way to a pile of brush at the end of a crude path. He moved the brush and kicked a layer of dirt to the side, exposing a thick piece of plywood. The plywood covered the opening of an underground tunnel.

"Come on," said Quang. "It's an old Viet Cong hospital and tunnel complex."

"You two go. I'll get the rest of the men," said Captain Minh.

Quang led Cao down a dirt stairway carved into the hard red soil about three feet wide and ten feet deep. A passageway about three feet high led to a room of about fifteen by fifteen feet square. Rough pine timbers lined the walls and supported the ceiling that was only six feet high. They crawled through the passageway and entered the room.

"This used to be an emergency room," said Quang. "I found it years ago by accident."

As Cao's eyes grew accustomed to the dim light, he began to make out bundles and boxes filling the room. Quang picked up an old rubber poncho and unwrapped an M-16 tied in oily rags and covered with part of an old Marine poncho liner. He handed it to Cao. The room was full of equipment wrapped in various protective ways.

"I have everything we need," Quang said. "Helmets, gun belts, flak jackets."

"Flak jackets?" exclaimed Cao. "How did you get this stuff?"

"I robbed or traded over the years," said Quang. "I felt someday it might be worth a lot of money on the black market."

Cao patted Quang on the shoulder.

"You and I need to talk."

The squad soon formed a human chain passing a rifle, helmet, magazine belt and flak jacket for each man through the narrow passage way and into the daylight. They moved with speed and precision and soon were ready to move out.

All the while Captain Minh's mind was working into the future. He pictured his own private little army forming in front of his eyes.

* *

Jim drove onto the bridge beyond the police checkpoint not knowing what to expect from the police guards. As he proceeded, he noticed the red and white barrier pole pulled down in place, but the checkpoint seemed to be deserted.

"Slow down," said Larry.

Jim slowed the black car and stopped just short of the barrier. Larry and Jim looked around and saw no one. The village ahead looked deserted. The market was closed, and the people were gone.

Yvonne spoke from the back seat. "Why don't you raise the barrier so we can get out of here?"

"I don't like this," said Larry. "You still have Chi Woo's gun?"

"Yes. Right beside me," said Jim.

"I guess nobody's here, Jimbo. Cover me anyway," said Larry as he drew his handgun and opened the car door.

Larry got out slowly and walked cautiously toward the barrier. He looked at the guard office, but could see no one. Putting his gun in his waistband, he started to lift the barrier.

"Drop the gun, Mr. Brewster!" came a loud voice.

Larry was startled and stepped backward into a mud puddle, and then noticed Summerpot stepping out of the guard shack with his own handgun carefully aimed at Larry.

"Summerpot, you old fool," said Larry. "Look what you made me do. My shoes are a mess."

Summerpot looked as Larry was stepping out of a small puddle of leftover rainwater. He noticed Larry's fancy shoes with the shiny brass buckles all covered in red mud.

"A pity, I'm sure," said Summerpot, "But put your gun down."

"For God's sake, Summerpot! Put your gun down. Larry saved us from Chi Woo," yelled Jim from the car as he put Chi Woo's pistol in his pant pocket.

The fat man stepped closer toward Larry.

"You don't understand my boy," returned Summerpot. "None of you do!"

Yvonne, Dr. Chin, and Mrs. Diem got out of the car, followed by Jim.

"Now, Mr. Brewster. For the third time, throw your gun on the ground."

Mrs. Diem moved closer to Summerpot as Yvonne tried to stop her. Larry started to comply when the police truck approaching from the other end of the bridge distracted the group. Larry seized the moment and knocked the gun out of Summerpot's hand and toward the feet of Yvonne's grandmother. A struggle ensued, and Jim joined Larry in subduing Summerpot. Larry struck the fat man across the face and drew his gun.

"Leave him be," screamed Mrs. Diem in Vietnamese as she picked up Summerpot's gun. She pointed it at Larry and Jim.

"Grandmother," yelled a shocked Yvonne, in Vietnamese. "Give me the gun."

"Don't do it, Mai," returned Summerpot, in Vietnamese.

The police truck had stopped a hundred fifty feet away and the two thugs and Lieutenant Nguyen got out in firing position, trying to make sense of what they were seeing.

"Leave him be," yelled Yvonne's grandmother again and this time she pointed the gun in the air and fired a round to everyone's shock and surprise.

The thugs and Lieutenant Nguyen thought the shot was fired at them and all three returned fire. Summerpot jerked and screamed in pain as a bullet hit his right shoulder. Jim started to turn and fell to the ground in pain, blood flowing from his right calf.

Larry let go of Summerpot and grabbed the gun from Mrs. Diem, knocking her down behind the front of the car. Yvonne dived back into the rear seat of the black sedan and took cover. Dr. Chin crouched behind the open front door. The brief shooting stopped.

"Throw down your weapons," the lieutenant called out.

Jim crawled over to Larry in front of the car. Summerpot was down and unconscious. Mrs. Diem was screaming at him in Vietnamese.

Larry pushed Summerpot's gun into his waistband and turned to Jim.

"Where's Chi Woo's gun?" asked Larry.

"Larry, I've been shot in the leg."

"Where's his gun, damn it," said Larry again.

Jim was shocked by Larry's tone.

"In my pocket," said Jim.

"Give it to me…"

Jim hesitated, confused by Larry's tone.

"Give it to me, damn it."

"Okay," replied Jim, as he fumbled for the gun in his pocket. His got it out and handed it to Larry. Larry placed it next to the other gun in his waistband. He turned to Dr. Chin.

"Get in the car, Dr. Chin," ordered Larry.

"What?" asked a startled Dr. Chin.

"Get in the car, Dr. Chin, or I'll blow that pretty daughter of yours away," threatened Larry.

Yvonne couldn't hear what was being said, but sensed something wrong.

Meanwhile, on the bridge, the lieutenant turned to the nearest thug. "Give me your rifle," he said.

Jim, in disbelief at what he had just heard, said, "Larry, what the hell's going on?"

"Sorry, Jimbo. I told you to stay out of this back in Bangkok. I tried to get you to drop it. I don't want to hurt anyone, but this is business. They just want the process."

Larry called to Dr. Chin again, telling him to get into the car. The doctor rushed into the front seat closing the passenger door behind him. Larry would be forced to run out in the line of fire to get to the driver's seat and make his getaway. He readied two of the handguns and turned to Jim.

"I'll try to make this up to you, Jimbo," he said.

Lieutenant Nguyen set himself, set the rifle to semiautomatic, and took aim, waiting for a clean shot at the tall white man with the gun.

Larry made his move. He jumped up firing both pistols and made a dash for the car door, but the lieutenant calmly squeezed off a round hitting Larry in the chest. He fell back toward Jim, and Jim pulled him back so that he was in front of the black sedan. Yvonne's grandmother had moved to the unconscious Summerpot and was lying over him.

The thugs fired a few more rounds, hitting the car and breaking a window. The lieutenant held their fire, sensing no fight was left. They proceeded slowly toward the car.

Jim heard a car racing down the hill behind them and turned to see an old green panel truck pull to a screeching halt. He was surprised to see Cao and Quang jump out of the front seat. He was even more surprised to see them in flak jackets. They took cover behind the truck's open doors and pulled out M-16s and helmets.

On the bridge, the lieutenant and the thugs saw the scene in front of them and started a retreat.

The old blue Peugeot pulled up behind the green panel truck and Captain Minh got out. He headed to the back door of the truck and opened it. The squad deployed out the back and moved to the bridgehead, two to a side, and took cover.

Captain Minh joined Cao.

"How do you want proceed Captain?" said Cao.

"I suppose I should try to get them to surrender first. If not, take them," said the captain.

Cao turned to Quang and called to him from between the open doors. "Quang, stay here and provide cover fire if I advance."

Quang nodded.

"Okay Captain," Cao said. "Your call now."

Captain Minh started to stand in hopes of offering a chance to surrender and as he did a burst of AK-47 fire strafed the truck door.

The captain fell to the red dirt, smashing the three cigars he had in his breast pocket.

"Take that asshole," the captain said.

"Cover fire," screamed Cao, and he took off right up the center of the road firing his M-16 like it was twenty-five years ago.

Two of the squad joined him while the other two poured fire on the police truck. Quang fired from the panel truck.

The thugs and the lieutenant couldn't muster a return of fire for fear of getting shot, and Cao and his men covered the distance in less than ten seconds. The two thugs and the lieutenant lay dead on the bridge without having fired another shot. Captain Minh rose up from behind the panel truck door. He looked at the old woman who was crying over Summerpot and at Dr. Braden holding on to his wounded friend.

"It's over everyone," he called out. "Hold your fire."

Yvonne jumped from the car and ran to her Grandmother. Dr. Chin got out and saw to Jim. Captain Minh was lighting a damaged cigar and the squad was returning from the bridge clearing their weapons. The captain smiled at Cao, very pleased with his work.

"Grandmother, are you okay?" asked Yvonne, wondering why she protected Summerpot after he sold them out.

"I'm fine," said the old woman.

Summerpot was coming around. He saw the old woman and took her hand in his. They hugged. Yvonne was confused.

"Are you all right, Mr. Summerpot?" asked Yvonne not sure what was going on between him and her grandmother.

"Yes, I believe it went through cleanly," said the fat man. "I seem to be breathing without difficulty."

"See to your friend," said her grandmother. "He is wounded."

"What?" Yvonne turned to look at Jim. "James!"

Yvonne dashed over to Jim and Larry.

"James, are you okay?" she asked, hugging him.

Cao and Quang came over and knelt by Jim and Larry. Cao took possession of Larry's guns.

"Jim, you okay," asked Quang.

"I should be, but Larry is hurt bad."

Cao looked at Jim's leg and placed a bandage.

"Hey, boss. You'll be okay. Just like old times at Thuong Duc."

"Huh?" said Jim.

"We'll tell you later," said Quang.

"You sit still, and we'll take care of your friend quick," said Cao.

Larry had been breathing erratically all through this conversation with a sucking chest wound and turned to Jim.

"Hey, Jimbo," Larry whispered. "I wasn't going to hurt her."

Cao placed some foil over Larry's wound and taped it shut. Then he took a bandage from a first aid kit on his magazine belt and tended to Jim.

"Jimbo, you liked me a little, didn't you?" whispered Larry.

"Sure, Larr. We all did."

"Bullshit!" said Larry. "I know the guys in the unit thought I was a loser, but I showed them. I was a big man in Bangkok, Jimbo. I just didn't want to lose that."

"It's okay, Larry. Be quiet now and save your strength," said Jim.

Yvonne and her father got up and returned to Mrs. Diem who had Summerpot sitting up. One of the squad was placing a bandage near the collarbone. Yvonne eyed the pair suspiciously.

"Mr. Summerpot! Who are you?" asked Yvonne.

Captain Minh, fighting his cigar, walked over and stood next to them.

"Allow me, Miss Chin," said Captain Minh. "Let me introduce you to your mother's father."

"What!" said Yvonne and Dr. Chin simultaneously.

"It's true my dear," said a subdued Summerpot. "At one time this woman next to me was the light of my life. In those days of early Nationalism a Vietnamese woman and a European man were frowned upon, as you well know, Dr. Chin. Our lives were so different, but we loved each other deeply. However, it was not to be. I left for her sake, and I did not find out about your mother, Michele, until years later. By then it was too dangerous and too late. Alas, I never met her."

"You're my real grandfather then…grandfather. It seems so strange to say it," said Yvonne. "And you really didn't sell us out."

"Well, I hope it's not too much of a shock," said Summerpot. "And no, I had to play along with Chi Woo to find out why he wanted you."

"After it was confirmed who you were, he would not let me rest," added Captain Minh.

"You know, years ago your grandmother got word to me about helping a little French Vietnamese girl reunite with her father. She never told me it was my granddaughter and son-in-law."

Yvonne and her father looked at one another and then at the older couple. It was almost too fantastic to believe.

"Mr. Summerpot," said Dr. Chin. "You're a brave and valiant man. Michele would have been proud of you."

Jim was still beside Larry as he listened to the conversation next to him. He looked down at Larry, after a moment, and found him staring straight up to the sky, eyes wide open. Jim laid a hand on his chest. It didn't move.

"Ah, Larry, not this way, not here after all these years," sighed Jim to his dead friend.

"Sorry, boss," said Cao. "We'll put him in the truck."

The rangers put Larry in the back of the panel truck and removed their fighting gear. They dumped the bodies of the thugs and the lieutenant in the back of the police truck and drove it off the bridge. Captain Minh would later say Lieutenant Nguyen died killing drug gangsters and would bury him with honors.

Summerpot and Jim were helped to Thanh's Peugeot, and Yvonne came over to talk to Jim.

"Miss Chin, do you think we can have that drink now?" asked Jim. "And dinner too."

Yvonne kissed him on the cheek.

"James, you been wonderful, but I have to get my father to safety, well away from Asia. Now I have my grandmother to worry about also, since they know who she is as well. It's too dangerous for her to stay in Thuong Duc anymore. Captain Minh will drive us in Chi Woo's car to the airport and we will take the first flight to anywhere out of the country."

"Yvonne, I'm in love with you," said Jim.

"James, it's not meant to be."

"Can't you give me something to grasp onto?" pleaded Jim.

She kissed him again and held his head with her hands.

"Maybe some day."

* *

# Chapter 13

Jim had just finished putting on real clothes for the first time in two weeks. His fractured fibula was healing, and he finally had a walking cast. The DaNang hospital was nice, but he was anxious to get going home. As he began packing his things, Summerpot strolled into the room followed by Captain Minh. Jim turned to them and smiled.

"It seems that every time I get ready to leave this country, they have to take a piece of metal out of me somewhere. They're never going to believe this back home."

"Well, personally, I prefer the casino to the hospital any time," said Summerpot.

"You're looking well," said Jim

"Yes, the million dollar wound. No bones or major organs hit," said Summerpot.

"You two should be more like me," said Captain Minh, while lighting a cigar.

"Keep away from gunfire altogether. I leave that to my officers and men like Cao and his squad."

"By the way, thank you for the way you've helped Cao and Quang these past two weeks," said Jim.

"My pleasure. Cao and Quang have become important men to me of late. Their talents will help keep me an important man in this city," said the captain.

"Yes, especially when the western nations start invading you economically," added Summerpot. "You see, my boy, Tran has aspirations of becoming a rich man. He and I are going to buy up as much of China Beach as the communists, in their quest for U.S. dollars, will let us buy, and build luxury hotels and condos. And rich men need faithful bodyguards."

"Speaking of Cao and Quang, they were supposed to be here by now. That plane won't wait for me," said Jim.

"Oh, they're both here. The whole squad is here. They're waiting for you outside. They have a surprise for you," said Captain Minh.

"A surprise, what is it?" asked Jim.

"You must wait and see. I can tell you it involves that large sum of money you gave them, plus an advance from me. The whole squad has become more important men because of it."

"Dr. Braden, if you're ready we can be off," said Summerpot.

"I'm all packed," said Jim.

An orderly was called and picked up Jim's bags as the three friends walked out of the hospital, Jim on crutches.

"So, Summerpot, other than the real estate deal what are your plans?" asked Jim

"I promised Yvonne that I would handle the sale of her antique shop," said Summerpot. "She has given me power of attorney and so I will go to Bangkok shortly. As far as anyone there is concerned, they still think I helped Chi Woo, and they think that Lieutenant Nguyen killed him and the other gangsters, thanks to Captain Minh."

"What about Yvonne? Have you heard from her?" asked Jim.

"No, my boy. I'm sorry things didn't work out, but we must respect her privacy," said Summerpot.

"I'm sorry, too," said Captain Minh. "I'm sorry you're her grandfather, and I'm depressed that I will never be able to enjoy her beauty as it was meant to be enjoyed."

"I rather imagine that the women of DaNang will bring you out of your depression before long," said Summerpot.

Just then a beautiful nurse walked by and smiled at the captain. He turned to watch her walk away. Summerpot and Jim made eye contact.

"I rather imagine it won't be long at all," laughed Jim.

They were all smiles as they walked out of the hospital entrance into the sunshine. Jim saw the cab squad lined up in front of their newly painted and restored pedi-cabs. Quang was standing by a brand new 50cc motor scooter. The squad snapped to.

"Attention," ordered Cao.

Jim put his hand over his eyes to block the bright sun. "What the heck?"

Cao, Quang, and the rest of the squad were standing at attention with very new and smart uniforms of shirts, shorts, knee socks, sandals, and caps.

"You like, boss?" asked Cao.

"Yes, I like," said Jim.

"Good! One more thing," said Cao.

Captain Minh leaned over and whispered in Jim's ear.

"Humor them. They have gone to a lot of work these past two weeks."

The squad moved their cabs out in a line so Jim could see the backs of all the bikes. There, in freshly painted colors, on the back of each cab, Jim saw the lettering: *BRADEN"S BIKERS, est. 1992.*

Jim roared with laughter at the sight.

"They took the money and purchased their cabs," said Captain Minh. "Then they refinished them. Quang has become my personal assistant and guardian of my private collection of U.S. Marine combat gear. I traded him for the scooter."

"Cao, Quang, this is great," said Jim, as he embraced each man.

Cao took Jim by the shoulders and looked into his eyes. Quang was close and smiling.

"Tell him," Quang said.

"Tell me what?" Jim said.

Cao paused and spoke to Jim.

"One more thing, Corporal Braden," said Cao. "I never suspected, but when Quang and I were driving to your rescue I asked him how he knew you. He still had that picture of you two, twenty-five years ago, that he took from your bag earlier that day. When he showed it to me, I knew who you both were. I am Ranger Sergeant Vien, the sergeant you always came to see when you needed to tell Quang something important."

"You're kidding!" said Jim.

"No, it's true," interrupted an excited Quang.

"Jim, you have given me and my men our self respect back. We will never forget you," said Cao, and they embraced again.

"Well, we'd better be going," Summerpot said.

Jim, Summerpot, and Captain Minh got into separate cabs, and the group peddled away led by Quang on his motor scooter. They arrived at the airport about ten minutes later, and the captain and Jim got out. They said their goodbyes once again and Jim hugged Cao and Quang, promising to write them and return again someday.

"Goodbye, my boy," said Summerpot.

"Goodbye, old friend," said Jim as they shook hands.

"I hope we both see *her* again someday," said Summerpot.

Jim and Captain Minh turned and walked toward the main terminal entrance, and the cab squad disappeared into the crowded street taking Summerpot back to his hotel. The two men walked in silence toward the customs center, and Jim finally spoke.

“I must admit that I never thought I’d ever be walking and talking with a NVA officer,” said Jim.

“Ex-officer,” said Captain Minh.

“Just the same it’s a strange feeling.”

“It doesn’t have to be. The Vietnamese people love America and want relations with it. When the time is right it will happen. You showed me a different side to the Rangers, perhaps I have shown you a different side to us from the north.”

At the customs center Captain Minh made sure Jim got through with no problems.

“Passport, please,” said the customs guard as he looked at the captain more than Jim.

Jim got out his passport and handed it to the guard who stamped it.

“No need to check his luggage,” said Captain Minh. “Send it through.”

“Thank you, my friend,” said Jim.

The captain nodded and shook Jim’s hand. As he watched Jim limp away, he reached for a cigar from his breast pocket.

Arriving at his gate, Jim saw a Boeing 747 Air France jet at the end of the jet way. He gave his ticket to the flight attendant who, to his disbelief, tore it up in front of him.

“What are you doing?” he demanded.

"Not to worry Dr. Braden," said the attendant. "Evidently someone in the flight center must have found out about your injury and upgraded you to first class. Let me help you to your seat."

"Wow, that's great," said Jim.

They worked their way down the ramp, through the door of the big plane, and started up the aisle in the business class section.

"Which seat is mine?" Jim asked.

"Right in front of the next bulkhead in the last row of first class."

Jim reached his seat in the back row and sat down stretching his cast leg out and closing his eyes. All of a sudden he was tired and ready to fly home to Seattle.

"Ah, that's better," he sighed.

"Would you like that drink now?"

"Pardon me?" said Jim; thinking it was the flight attendant's voice.

"Oh, my god, you came back," said Jim when he saw it was she.

He took Yvonne in his arms and kissed her passionately. She pulled away briefly for air and to get a word in.

"You promised me dinner, too," she said.

"You get more than that," Jim returned. "I'll give you the world."

# THE END

# ABOUT THE AUTHOR

In 1987 I returned to Vietnam for the first time where I actually met ex-rangers peddling cabs in DaNang. Their life was similar to the description I wrote in this book. These men actually took my ten companions and me all around the city for three days. We over paid them so they could afford a few luxuries like new clothes and food.

Our North Vietnamese handlers during that trip initially were annoyed by our payment, but they too loosened up and became good friends. One named Tran was an ex-NVA officer.

There was also a real bicycle race through the center of town.

I asked our handlers in 1987 if I could go out to Thuong Duc, but they said no one would drive me out their because they were afraid to go to the mountains.

I actually saw older American autos on that trip and an old blue Peugeot taxi.

In 2011 I returned to Thuong Duc with my number two son Jeff Cowart, Jack Wells, one of my Marine lieutenants from 1968, and fellow dentist, Ron Berquist.

Made in the USA
San Bernardino, CA
24 March 2016